I am you

-a novel by Kartikeya Sharma

For information, contact:

kartikeyakylansharmasmith@gmail.com

First Edition

Cover design by Kartikeya Sharma

Printed in India

Acknowledgements.

This book is a big step for both me and my career. I am so happy to finally complete this story. It was planned for around an year now and I have waited many months to write it and, in the end, here it is.

I have wonderful and amazing friends who encouraged me to make this book into existence. My first readers Bhakti Joshi and Abhinav Shukla, helped with the core of this book and really inspired and helped me along this journey. Other than those Virat Singh, Arnav Prakash Sharma, Shubham Sharma, Chhavi Sharma and Rudra Bharadwaj… you all are wonderful and really special to me. Thank you all

Coming to family, my parents, Manmohan Sharma and Neetu Sharma and my brother Vijjval offered endless support and advice on things I was missing out on. Love you all.

To my teacher, Ms. Guncha Khan… thank you very much for giving review of the base story and believing in me.

Subham Saini a.k.a. BeastBoyShub… If it wasn't for him this novel would've never existed. I came to know from his videos about an anime which heavily inspired me to think of a story like this. Thank you very much sir.

Special thanks to the song 'Die for you' by STARSET… a wonderful song which really pushed me to the doors of my imagination, I still remember those late nights when I used to listen to this song and think about the story.

I am you.

Chapter 1

- The Longing

The early morning sunlight filtered through the curtains of my room, casting a warm glow over my desk, which was filled with textbooks, sketches, and comic books. I sat on the edge of my bed, staring at the wall like everyone does. The day ahead felt like just another routine, of which I was **TIRED**. "Another day, another round of pretending that everything is fine, and I haven't eaten some old amla."

I dragged myself out of my bed and tried to think of something good that could happen today, "Shit, I forgot to do my Hindi homework… eh, either way the teacher just ignores me, I've had a good image of myself in front of her"

I never procrastinated to go to bath even in the month of November, just that I cursed myself every time I go in the bathroom. I got out, sprayed some cologne and deodorant, got dressed in my uniform with full efficiency.

"Of course… I was used to it."

I made my way to the dining table; my mom greeted me with a smile. "Good morning son! I've made your favorite parathas… quickly eat up, I must go to pick up your father from the station, he's coming back today."

It made my face lit up, he was my idol, a hardworking, family man who didn't teach me to stand any sort of despicable, sly and wicked people… Sure I was suspended from school for 2 days because I was too much for a group of nine people, one of them had his hand fractured, I sometimes wonder if he was just pretending or I am actually this strong. I knew for a fact my father never punished me for it, he was proud of me, I protected my friend from the gang whose leader was the brother of the girl who had a crush on him. Sounds complicated right? I'll tell you that after I've understood it myself.

I am you.

"Thank you, mom" I greeted her and finished the parathas with a forced smile, not like I didn't like parathas, but I was stressed because of the extensive 10th grade routine. I ate quickly; my mind wasn't on my food but on the day ahead.

Oh, and what do you know? My thoughts drifted to my 'lady love' no not my girlfriend, I just liked her, for 2 YEARS… Nandini, Nandini Rathore, she occupied my every waking moment. She was smart, charming and VERY beautiful, but despite my best efforts, I always felt like there's a wall between us, one I could never break through and NO I was not scared to talk to her… who am I kidding of course I was scared to talk to her.

I finished my food, combed my hair for the fourth time after bath, packed my bag, took my earphones and MP3 player, just kidding I took my phone. I wore my shoes and went on my way to school through the cold November winds.

I always enjoyed my walks, listening to music, thinking about my dreadful life, or exams are coming closer. My earphones were playing energetic beats, and I was gliding my way through the cold winds. My focus landed on a couple sitting on a bench, both reading a book, in each other's arms. The song in my mind started to fade as I looked at their intimacy. Soon after I spotted a group of friends on their morning walk, their laughs and jokes filled the air. "When will I get to enjoy this type of life?" I questioned myself; I kept thinking of jokes in my head, took everything very lightly and kept adding something that would make me or at least others laugh, but it wasn't me inside. I wanted to enjoy my life.

I reached my school after a few minutes; the halls were bustling with energy, and the teachers were preparing for the day. I walked into the class after climbing three floors, "Who made these stairs out of marble? Always make me lose my traction on turns." Yes, I was a GT3 fan as well. Two of my closest friends, Nikhil and Aditya joined me. They were talking about yesterday's cricket match, but I wasn't interested in it, so I was unable to fully engage. YES, I am an Indian and don't watch cricket matches, cut some slack I already have many interests on my plate.

I am you.

Nikhil, as always, kept blabbering, "Did you see the six Dhoni hit? Unbelievable!", "Yea and the catch at the boundary? Insane!", Aditya replied to him.

"You came from two rows behind just to talk about the IPL match?" I continued "What the actual hell is wrong with you?!"

"Oh, yea we forgot this dumbass doesn't watch IPL, or any other sports" Nikhil yapped, as he always does. "I can say the same for you that you play just TWO video games and that too what I gave you, so Shut it!" Yes, I am a gamer as well, don't mind me.

Now… I appreciated their friendship, they were my home boys but sometimes I felt like an outsider among them, they could talk for hours about cricket, western movies or other things that happened on discord last night, but I often found myself craving something deeper, something more meaningful. I wasn't completely sure of what I wanted exactly, but at that time, a donut for sure, CHOCOLATE, no strawberry… GOD I HATE STRAWBERRIES! "Hey, I am going to roam around, if u guys want you can come alright" I said this as I was leaving the class.

As I roamed the corridors, my eyes scanned the crowd for Nandini and there she was, standing with her friends, laughing at something someone had said, my heart gave a familiar lurch, but I knew better than to approach her just yet. People always surrounded her, and I never quite knew how to insert myself in her world; EVEN though I knew everything about her like her favorite food, topics, color, drink, her height, her weight, her shoe size, hair type everything. How did I know it? My observing and listening skills can sometimes be handy and NO I AM NOT A STALKER like my friends call me sometimes.

"AN OX IS BEHIND YOU!" Aditya nudged me so hard I was about to shout like a girl being kidnapped.

"Go talk to her already, you have been pinning over her for months now." Years but he wouldn't know it, he became my friends just last year, "And it's not that easy, I don't know why but my confidence disintegrates

I am you.

as soon as I see her" Of course, like every little teenager;
I hate myself sometimes.

Nikhil approached with a wide smile on his face,
"Let me just tell her myself." And before he knew it a
flying slap hit his face hard. He became furious but of
course he knew he was no competition to me unless I let
him win, smart boy. Now… it was not just about
impressing Nandini- it was about finding someone who
could understand me, someone who can see beyond the
surface… and because she was gorgeous. Being a friend
of hers for 1 year made me believe that she could be the
one, plus her charm just enveloped me. "Come on
Krishay, just go and try to, uhm…" Try to what huh?
Nikhil had not even talked to her 4-year-old crush, and
he was giving ME advice.

"Let us just go all right. Class is about to start"
and we went back to our classroom… Shit, our teacher
was already there, we are doomed.

The day passed in a blur of classes and idle
chatter; I usually sit with Aditya with Nikhil behind us. I
was doodling in my notebook while our teacher

blabbered about Mole Concept. I glanced over at Nandini a few times, but she was engrossed in her own world, chatting with her friends, or taking notes with intense focus which I admired. "Snap out Krish, focus on studies" … I was a bit frustrated, "You do know I get better grades that you or Nandini right?"

During the lunch break, Nikhil and Aditya were in their usual high spirits and I being the "Hero of class" found myself zoning out again. I was staring at the school yard out from the window, watching as groups of students laughed and joked with each other, without caring about the world. NO, it wasn't that I was alone or what you all must have been thinking, 'Ungrateful'- I had good friends, other that these two rats as well, but there was a disconnect, like something was missing… maybe I am just a bit autistic or the fact I am so unique I am considered abnormal now, like an abomination who is a gamer and nerd.

I wish there were someone out there who really got me, someone who was like… me.

I am you.

"Hey Krishay! Wanna join us?" right in the middle of my daydreaming session, Nandini called out my name from the opposite row.

Everyone in class started staring at me with a mischievous smile and giggling around like hyenas. I went to the group where she was standing, I saw Nikhil on my right, he had the biggest smile on his face with a specific pride. I knew it! That bastard told Nandini to involve me as well.

Now I was that desperate guy who doesn't know how to talk in front of her. The group was three girls and two boys excluding me. I was getting into the talks when this guy Rohit looked at me with a judging look and put the effort opened his mouth to ask the weirdest question…

"Hey so, I think we missed on introductions don't you think?" WE ARE IN THE SAME FRICKING CLASS, and it's already been eight months, how do you not know my name, but I was glad he asked it because now I can say the lines I have been preparing for a while…

Kartikeya Sharma.

"Leader of my trio, artist by passion, first born in my house, I... am... Krishay Sharma."

And at that time, I knew two things, either I nailed this line and now everyone including Nandini likes me, or it was just cringe and everyone thinks that I am just an immature Bollywood fan.

To my surprise, it wasn't that bad, in fact I could see that Rohit was jealous of me, and I immediately understood, "He also wants to ask out Nandini!" Now I was incredibly happy that I delivered the line, because now everyone was shocked at my unexpected intro. I had bubbles of happiness bursting inside me, "Oh YES! I did it, I made a great first not first impression on Nandini, Suck it ROHIT! You are nowhere near the ambience of Krishay... Thank you Shiva, let the school be over I'll buy some sweets for you."

"Oh, wow you are no less than a movie star" Nandini held my shoulder while giving this amazing compliment which melted me inside out. "What shall I

I am you.

do, I am just like this" The girls returned to the talk, and
I was just staring at Nandini, seeing which I am sure
Rohit was burning his ass as if he had eaten taco bell.
The other dude Ranjeet was just chill, he didn't talk
much but he sure clapped for me. In a sentence I was
happy to make Nandini and others smile and Rohit
jealous.

As the final bell of the day rang, I packed my
things and walked out of school. I was about to leave the
campus when a girl shouted my name and came running
towards me, no it wasn't Nandini, it was Rupali Bakshi,
the girl I met during a joint event.

"Hi K! Wanna grab an ice cream?

I really wasn't in a mood and didn't really care
but, "Sure, I can get one, Thanks!"

When we both we standing against a wall eating
our ice cream, I was constantly thinking about one or the
other thing, studies, Nandini, music et cetera. I glanced
at Rupali, and she was already looking at me from the
corner of her eye, "What happened, is everything alright"

Kartikeya Sharma.

I asked her, in a desperate attempt to break the silence. Huh, why did I do it?

"Oh, uh, um nothing, just… nothing" She fumbled like crazy! Her cheeks flushed with embarrassment and her eyes down on the ground. Before she knew I quickly finished up my ice cream, threw the stick and greeted her a goodbye with a gentle smile, "Thank you once again, I'll look forward to our next hangout." Nah I won't probably, I mean she was not a bad girl by any means, just I am not in a mood for random hangouts right now. I never am.

While reaching home I decided to go to my favorite café, *32 Apples*. I went inside and suddenly all the waitresses waved and greeted at me. I came here quite often…

This place has great aesthetics, scents and the food… just chef's kiss. "Hi Krishay, your usual?" the cashier asked me. My usual is a cold Vanilla latte.

"Yes Sharon, and please put a bit more whipped cream today, I'll pay extra if I have to." She immediately started working on it and in no time, I had my latte in my hands.

I am you.

"Good as always." It was a place where I can freely relax and stop thinking about all the people or studies, and a break from this heat which I don't know how it is possible in November in North India.

"Global Warming issues." I whispered while enjoying my latte in peace.

I reached home not realizing my father was already there, I bowed and touched his feet to seek his blessings. "Live long and stay happy son, what are you up to?"

"Nothing much, studies, boredom and all" We talked a good fifteen minutes and then I went in my room to change. That night I lay on my bed, my mind was wandering again in a distinct world- one where I wasn't alone in my thought, where someone out there was JUST like me, caring, introvert, strong, stunning, cool, funny... just perfect. It was a silly thought, but it brought me a sense of comfort. I was also thinking about today's incident.

"I loved it today; it was so perfect like they show in movies. I delivered a speech, and everyone was amazed by it, NANDINI was impressed by it, but is she even worth it though? I mean yea she is nice and all but, is she the person who is like me? Oh, absolutely not, I am a depressed nerd, and she is a lively, free dove."

I relaxed my mind and just whispered before my eyes shut closed,

"Maybe someone out there is a person… someone who truly understands me. I am tired of just observing and understanding others."

I am you.

Chapter 2

-A picture in mind

In the middle of a particularly dull afternoon, the students were bored and causing havoc while our English teacher, Mrs. Tripathi just stood there trying to somehow quiet them down… I was just talking about the most bullshit stuff with my friends. Mrs. Tripathi decided to take a break from the regular curriculum to tell us a story; she asked for everyone's attention.

"Students, today I want to tell you a story which I wrote back when I was in high school like you all."

She began pacing slowly at the front of the room. "It's about a forty-five-year-old man, living in a world after an apocalypse, everything and everyone he knew was gone and he was utterly alone."

My ears perked up as I heard the word "alone". I shifted my seat, focusing on our teacher. "To keep his sanity" she continued,

"This man decided to draw a person. He poured his heart into the sketch, creating someone who would be his companion in that lonely world. "Why won't he just die!" That was Harshita, the most annoying girl in our whole school, most likely. As soon as she said that a girl slapped her shutting her up, we were relieved.

"Overtime, this drawing became his only friend, the only thing that kept him going. Even though it was just a picture, it was as if the person really existed for him, giving him strength and hope."

The room was silent, students hanging on Mrs. Tripathi's every word and Krishay was mesmerized. The idea of creating someone who could be there for him, someone who understood him even in his solitude, struck a deep chord within him.

As soon as the bell rang, signaling the end of the period and the school, I was out of his seat in a flash. Nikhil and Aditya called after me, puzzled by my sudden rush.

"Hey, where are you going? We were supposed to go eat Gol Gappe."

I am you.

"I'll catch up with you guys later… probably not."

I ran through the corridor only to find my senior wing coordinator Mrs. Vyaas, walking in front of me. In a sudden jerk, I preferred to slip down than letting her know I was running. I put my hand down and slipped across the marble and came to an end by stopping myself against a table. Good thing she thought I just fell on the ground.

I greeted her and slowly jogged to the stairs. I ran the entire way home, bursting through the front door and headed straight to my room.

As soon as I was about to grab my sketch book and pencil, a flying substance, primarily made up of rubber, used as melee as well as for ranged, primarily used in Asian households, commonly called a "slipper" or "flip flops" came right at my face.

Nah just kidding but she did scream at the top of her lungs, "KRISHAY! Have you lost your mind? You didn't change your clothes, didn't wash hands, didn't get fresh, didn't eat food and just went to draw? Your exams are also coming, did you forget? I swear I'll rip this book off."

With a stare she left my room, I groaned in anger but knew she was right. I went to take a cold shower after all the running. "Ok so here's the plan, I eat my food, prepare the whole geography and then in the night I can sit to make my sketch" Damn you really think the best in shower. I ate my food and as planned, by 8pm I finished the whole subject.

After dinner I sat on my chair, took my book and pencil and started thinking. "Ok, this pose looks good, let's do it Krishay" I prayed to the photo of Shiva on the wall in front of me, as I always do before any work and started off with the basic figures. Nothing special for today just some references. "I am so excited to see how this will turn up! For now, it's already 1am, I should head to bed, or I'll be grumpy in the morning."

While lying on the bed, I was thinking how I'll make her, "If she'll be just like me, I shall take my reference from my face, and the name should be… uh, Ritisha? Priya? Nah I hate that name, Palak? Too general, Romsha? Unique but, eh… something like mine maybe,

I am you.

Krishay huh... Krishani...Kriti... KRITIKA! That's good, Kritika Sharma, I like this..." with that I excitedly and unwillingly drifted to sleep.

Since that day, I always woke up at 3 a.m. I've always been a night owl, but since then my nights took an unusual routine. As soon as I opened my eyes, I knew what I had to do. I'd quietly slip out of my bed, making sure not to make any noise that could wake my family. The house was silent, the world outside was still with only the noise of fan spinning. I loved this time; it felt like the world belonged to me.

I used to go downstairs, grab my favorite snack and then lock my room once I am in. I opened my laptop for some good music beating though my headphones in my ears. For the next hour, I'd be lost in my thoughts, my hand would move in a fluid motion.

I was creating nothing other than a girl, why not a boy? Everyone knows why. She only existed in my imagination. I had no hurry to finish it off, I'd spend weeks and months if required but I'd make her *perfect*.

Kartikeya Sharma.

Every night she became clearer, a little more real. I planned precisely on which day I'll make which of the features. It wasn't a small project; I had to tear countless pages. Some nights focused on her features, how her hair might fall, or how her lips should look when she smiles, it took me 4 days just to make her lips perfect, the main reason being they are the most attractive part of a female's face for me.

I imagined her personality to be like me, of course; kind yet strong, someone who would laugh easily but also knew when to be serious and *extremely* beautiful, like how handsome I am.

"I don't know why I do this, but it makes me happy."

This wasn't just a statement, after every session I felt a strange sense of peace, like I was getting closer to something I didn't fully understand. During the day, I couldn't stop thinking about her, not Nandini, Kritika. It was like she was a MUCH superior version of her, no offence to Nandini.

I'd find myself smiling for absolutely no reason, just lost in my thoughts. This "new habit" of smiling

I am you.

didn't go unnoticed. My friends were the first to pick up on it. Durning lunch Nikhil opened his tiffin box and approached me.

He was laughing at me, "Tell me one thing, what has gotten into you? Why are you smiling and laughing and lost since a couple days?"

"Look I just got three samosas instead of two!" Aditya came into the classroom jumping. "It was so crowdy and he accidentally gave me one extra! Although I am not giving it to any of you"

"Hey, we were to ask him of his disease remember?"

"Oh yes, right. What are you crazy or something?"

I was STILL lost in thoughts and could barely hear them, "Maybe I am."

Aditya's comedy mode turned on, which is for sure indication that he'd roast you, "Ah yes… that is your response. Let's say you are a dipshit moron, *yes I am,* your doctor tells you that you have explosive diarrhea, *maybe I have,* or you realize your girlfriend is an afro American slave who just wants to touch you, *maybe he is.*"

Nikhil was laughing like crazy; his mouth was big enough to fit a full guava.

The teachers also noticed the change too, I was often caught daydreaming in class, my thoughts were far away from the chapter Nervous System my Mrs. Chaturvedi was teaching.

"Krishay! Are you here or lost somewhere else?"

I snapped back to reality and offered my irresistible puppy face with my sweet smile. No kidding, I once got a free plate of dumplings when I didn't have money after I ordered them from the stall in front of school.

"Sorry ma'am, won't happen again." She was confused and I knew why was that "Won't happen again? This is the third time you have made this face! One more time and you are out of my class, then keep making this face in front of Mrs. Vyaas."

Despite my distractions, my grades didn't suffer at all, my father has taught me the importance of

I am you.

priorities. I know when to focus and when to absolutely set myself free. This was a shock for the teachers because they constantly told me that my grades would go down, they never did.

It was the "eyes and eyebrows" day. It was quite difficult for me to get the eyes of a human correct, so I knew it was going to be a long task. I made first eyes with some missing details like eye lashes and the small details in the iris, but it was already 4a.m. I shut down the laptop, put away the sketch and lay on my cozy bed.

I think many people will relate to it that when you work late at night and your back is absolutely violated, laying on the bed is the best feeling after that.

For some reason, making the sketch and the happiness it gave made me less scared in front of Nandini. I don't know, maybe I am just tripping. More than Nandini, I was thinking about Kritika which was crazy because I haven't even completed her face yet and she didn't have any voice.

Kartikeya Sharma.

Now when I woke up, I was not in my bed, it was a beaten-up sofa which smelled like old leather and cigarette smoke. It was a dull, dark and messed up apartment, kind of like Comic Deadpool. A dim light was flickering over me. I stood up in utter confusion, where was I?

The door creaked open and there was a woman standing there. Her body gave the resemblance of Kritika. She was coming close to me, but her face was covered with a dark shadow. My heart was beating fast, and I felt unusual fear, something dangerous about her. As she was about to come even closer, I jolted awake drenched in sweat. "It was a dream, dang it I could've seen how she looked."

I was thinking of the dream throughout the day, in class, at lunch everywhere, it was different, but in a scary way. My class teacher Mr. Tiwari stopped me during dispersal when I was going out.

He was very calm and concerned, "Krishay, is everything alright? You seem quite different these days, other teachers have noticed it as well." I knew he was caring about me but of course I was just fine, "I am fine sir, thanks for asking though."

He was confused because my face had no sign of either stress of classes or tension of exams. "Okay if you say so, but remember you can always share anything with me alright?"

Of course, I wasn't going to share I am scared to talk to Nandini, or I am obsessed over a girl who is just like myself… WHOM I HAVE CREATED. So, I just left. I was going through the ground and looking for my friends. I saw Rupali waving and walking towards me, "Great, I'll be late to home now."

"Hi K, looking for your buddies?"

"As a matter of fact, I am." She was always so lively and excited to see me, everyone told me that she likes me, but I wasn't going to judge her like that, I consider her my friend.

We were crossing the road when she started walking and since it was a single lane road, she didn't see the bike coming from the other way. I held her bag and pulled her back and how clumsy of her, she fell. At least she didn't get hurt by the bike.

"Will you help me or what?" Drama Queen, I reached my hand to help her get on her feet. Nikhil approached us and he put his hand across my shoulder, "We were finding you everywhere", I asked where Aditya was, "He went along with his other friends, it's just you and me… and you as well" he was talking about Rupali.

While we were walking Rupali asked me how my progress with Nandini was going, when Nikhil TRIED to give me some advice, "Bro you have to be mysterious to attract girls"

"Your crush still doesn't know you exist, THAT is the peak mystery and it's not working."

Rupali laughed so hard it drilled a hole through my tympanum. "Hey! She is not my crush anymore" I knew he'd say it, "Sure, whatever you say mystery man."

I bought a donut and was thinking, maybe it was enough, I had to take the step now… I said to both, "I am doing it tomorrow, I am asking her out on a small ice cream date."

I am you.

Nandini seemed quite and sad, but Nikhil was teasing me, "Now where is this confidence coming from, if it's the donut tell me, I'll also buy one right now" I don't know exactly why she didn't say anything, but I was more focused on the plan.

That night when I drew Kritika's neck details, I was talking to her, I might be crazy, "Tomorrow I am doing it girl, I will approach her when no one is around, but that's the problem, she is barely alone, maybe follow her when she goes to bathroom? Nah that's creepy."

"You shouldn't be afraid of how people will judge you, you've made a great impression on them already" yeah, I am definitely tripping, she is talking to me now, "Now get your butt tight, swallow that fear and ask her in front of her friends if it's necessary"

She told me, and I've made her, so I told it to myself, it's official… I am doing it tomorrow.

"Yeah, that's the spirit! Now go get her soldier…", Yeah sure but I'll do it after I sleep, good night.

Kartikeya Sharma.

That night I again woke up in that apartment, instead I was on the ground with all the beer spilling over the ground from the bottles. The lamp barely lit up anything and the T.V. was showing static. From the room inside, a lady walked over, I was terrified, I held a bottle in my hand for defense, "How can you do this Krishay?" She said in a soothing voice, "Wha… What do you mean?" I asked hesitantly.

"You created me, and you'll go out with another girl?" I was confused, "What are you talking about, you told me to go shoot my shot, last time I checked I didn't create you as a hypocrite."

She shook her head and went out of my sight, my vision blurred and as I tried to follow her, my alarm was off, it woke me up. It was too real and too strange, "Why am I dreaming such dreams?" Maybe tonight I should take a break from this sketching project.

Chapter 3

-Sketchy Business

I was still in a bit of shock, it wasn't like anything I have seen before, maybe it's just me getting too addicted to her. I quickly took a bath, brushed like never before and took a perfume bottle for school so I can use it before asking her out.

I ran to school full of excitement and nervousness… I thought to myself if I reached there early, I could ask her alone. I sped up but there it was, a tree fell on the ground due to the heavy winds last night. I wasn't going to give up, I turned on full vector mode and went from an alley.

It was closed so I climbed a car and then to the terrace of a house, I vaulted my way through the walls, jumping across water tanks and pipes. "Damn I never get to do these things now, made me remember the old times."

There was an old woman doing yoga, I slid past her, and she was not happy, why is that? She threw a fricking rock at me!

I jumped across two houses with death under me. "Still got those old moves."

I jumped across buildings and then got off on the other side of the road. The road was empty because of the tree but soon after I saw a bus turning from the corner behind me. I got an idea, I ran and hung on the ladder behind it, I saved precisely 23 minutes than how I would usually come to school.

I slowly climbed the stairs thinking of what would happen, "What if she just laughed, what if she said no, what if she said yes but it was just a prank."

I went to the bathroom first, I fixed my shirt and tie and removed the dirt from my blazer and pants, I took out the comb and made my hair and the atom bomb, my old spice scent. Now I am ready. As I was walking to my class, my fear was increasing, my heart was pounding, mostly due to breathlessness.

I am you.

"What if this is my last time asking a girl because then we will get along so good that we will eventually marry! Yea I should think of it like this. Wait, but what if she thinks I am a creep and she tells everyone in class, even worse, what if she tells Mr. Tiwari. Shit I'll be in so much trouble; my parents will kill me!"

I entered the room, there were very less people, it's a good thing, she was also there, talking to her friend Vaishnavi, "Ok Krish, you got this, stay confident, talk naturally, maintain your posture and remember, you are a Sharma, we don't back down from things.

I put my bag on the chair and approached her, she and her friend both looked at me, "What is happening? Why are my legs shaking, my heart is beating so fast!" I somehow gathered every ounce of courage left in my body to finally ask her, "Hey I was thinking about taking you to the market nearby and maybe we can get some ice cream, or anything else if you want, what do you say?"

Kartikeya Sharma.

My legs were so unstable I felt like I was going to fall, the time was going so slow, why won't she just reply already!

"Oh, I'd love to! Let's go after school, nevertheless we hardly get any time to talk to each other, I am so down."

SHE AGREED! I had a burst of adrenaline running through my nerves and I could feel it in my ears, they were burning like hell. "Okay, see you after school then" and I went outside the class to express my happiness… I had the biggest smile on my face, and everyone was looking at me as if I had won Mr. Beast's challenge.

Aditya came and I ran towards him, I *did not* jump and hugged him like girls would do, I held his shoulders and excitedly told him everything. "Oh finally, I was starting to believe you are attracted to men. So, is it official right?"

"Well not right now, I just asked her out after school" he was very excited listening to this, "Oh where are you going, Gol Market? I know a stall which sells the

I am you.

best biryani, or the Day Light Fish, it's a food truck and I
cannot describe how good his fried fish is."

"Yeah, actually we are just going to get some ice
cream, and she's vegetarian."

"Oh, ok" his face lost all the excitement, "then
go to the Gol Market and take the second left, there is an
ice cream shop, it'll be enough to make her happy." and
he just started walking to the class.

I saw Vaishnavi coming towards me, "What why
is she coming, did Nandini changed her mind? Did she
just agree back there to make me feel happy? I am about
to die of embarrassment!"

"Wow Sharma, that was smoother than I
expected" wait, what do you mean "expected"?

"Well, I knew you liked her, and actually I know
a lot of stuff about you, like you pretend to be all cutie,
but you are one hell of a fighter, that's the reason mostly
people who intimidate others don't talk to you, your
fight that time wasn't a secret for too long and that
Rupali has a big time crush on you."

Kartikeya Sharma.

Yea she's a witch, now she'll strangle me in the bathroom, and I'll be dead, goodbye mom and dad, "How did you get to know these things about me?"

"Well let's just say you're not the only one who can *observe* others… agent Night wing."

My face turned pale, "She knows my code name, how?" should I make her unconscious and stuff her in a closet? I've learned how to make chloroform; I just need to go to the chemistry lab. She started laughing and giggling, "Don't worry Mr. Sharma, I am not here to expose you, I just came here to tell you she also has something for you, if you move properly maybe she'll start to like you more, Good Luck alright."

"No wait" I stopped her, "Uh can you tell me, what do you mean by Rupali has a crush on me?"

"What's not to understand here, she is a girl, you are a boy, she has developed feelings for you, is it that hard to understand?"

I am you.

"Wait that shouldn't be right, you must be tripping" She immediately replied in the dullest tone ever, "K don't pretend you didn't know it."

"Ok you're right I knew, maybe I kept ignoring it because we won't get together anyway."

Yeah, whatever let's go to the class, sir is about to come. We both sat on our seats, I looked at Nandini and she was already looking at me! We both looked away in a split second, embarrassed, I started digging in my bag for something I wasn't sure of.

Finally, Nikhil came as well, "Hey sit down quick! I did it, I DID IT… I asked her out and she said yes!" Nikhil was in shock, as if he was stunned or sitting on a pencil. "Congratulations man, now tell me when I am becoming an uncle."

"First tell me when the wedding is because till that time, I need to get the Murcielago LP-640 so I can drift in your wedding and steal your bride."

We both gave Aditya concerning looks, "No use, I'll be having the BMW M3 GTR, in the Need for Speed: Most Wanted livery. "Ha, good luck with owning and importing the body kit, rims, roll-cage, exhaust and the big V8 for the swap before I do get my hands on my Murci…" he laughed in the end.

"You guys are competing who will have his car first and with whom Nandini will go rather than trusting her that she'll be loyal to Krish? You both are insane."

Aditya leaves no opportunity to pull Nikhil's underwear, "At least we are fighting for a girl, unlike you" They both started fighting again, I was finally thinking maybe my life is not so bad after all, I mean soon me and Nandini will be even closer, I couldn't contain my excitement that day.

In the middle of my biology class, our teacher was talking about dreams and their importance, it struck me, the dream from last night and before that. My focus shifted from the topic to the strange moments I experienced last night, I totally forgot about them, I was talking to a sketch. I started worrying about having a mental illness, I brushed it off thinking I may be sleepy, trying not to stress myself before my big moment.

It was lunch time, we opened our tiffin boxes and as we started to munch on Nikhil's pasta, Nandini

I am you.

and Vaishnavi were passing through our seat, they both were looking at me and smiling, I never felt this good ever before, it was like I was having the world in my hand…

"Go talk to her she's indicating you to do it!" Nikhil tried to push me out of my seat which I ABSOLUTELY hate… like that guy hasn't had a single relationship of his own and he's giving *me* relationship advice? "I'll be really happy if you showed this courage in front of your crush… what was her name again?"

"Parvati? Palak? Oh, right it was Paarvi" Don't judge Aditya, he sometimes remembers names like an AI and sometimes like a goldfish. "Hey! Don't say it out loud, and she's not my crush anymore."

"That's because you don't have any chance yea I know. It's been like this for like 2 years now and I honestly feel like she has filed a freaking restraining order against you" I said with a small laugh. Now as always, Nikhil tried to brag about his 'flirting' skills. I laughed so hard the students were all staring at me… luckily Nandini wasn't there or else something would've happened… something not very appealing.

Kartikeya Sharma.

After finishing our lunches, I went outside to look for her… just to look at her because she was definitely in some other class talking to her friends. I don't even know how you make so many friends and actually stay in contact with them. I was walking through the hall looking for her in every class, I couldn't find her. I asked one of her friends who was passing by and she just giggled and walked away.

"You don't have to be mean" just as I said it while turning back, there she was, behind me, giving me a sign to say what I wanted to say, I gave her a gritty sign pretending that I wasn't looking for her but of course she wasn't buying it, I was having a mental breakdown when suddenly Mr. Tiwari called me, I was relieved and I just went as fast as possible.

He asked me to come to the library to help him with some assignment sheets. On the way there, the lunch break was over, we had to walk down 2 floors and then climb one floor of the other building of our school. Apparently, they were too cheap to connect those two buildings which were literally adjacent to each other. Sir

I am you.

told me to look for a blue folder in a red crate in the library storage room, the place was so dark even the sunlight couldn't enter it, well that's probably because it had no windows but, it was just too dark.

"Can I get your phone? For the flashlight" I asked him while he was talking to the librarian about some school stuff. At first, I went to the 12th grade section, I realized it when none of the students' name was heard by me... I started putting those away and suddenly in my mind, last night's dream popped up. That dirty apartment, the feeling that I am in a condition worse than Deadpool himself. More than that I got an urgent urge to complete Kritika's sketch, "Now only her body and a few details are left, it should be complete in a day or two."

My thinking was a mistake, sir scolded me that the 10th grade section was on the other side... I quickly got the papers, and we went to the classroom. Apparently, I spent so much time in there that half of the class was over, Mr. Tiwari could only hand us our sheets with grades but couldn't explain the next topic, it was a win-win.

39

Kartikeya Sharma.

I waited and waited till finally what felt like 2 years, the bell finally rang. I quickly packed my bag, but I realized that it would make me seem desperate, so I started talking to Nikhil and Aditya while slowly packing my bag. I am usually one of the guys in class who runs outside the classroom very first, I just *can't* bear crowds. Even if my friends are still in the classroom, I just wait for them outside the school. This time it was different; I was waiting for her to go before me, so it feels like I am not desperate to go out with her, which in reality I really am.

"I am going to make this worth it, trust me Nandini" I said it but not with my usual confidence, I didn't know but I was unsure of something, I didn't know of what, but I just felt a feeling that something is off.

I am you.

Chapter 4

-The Date

I reached the ground, I asked Aditya and Nikhil to continue on their way home without me.

"Hey, are you ready?" I got this question from behind me; it was her, "Oh… yes, yes let's go" She greeted goodbye to her friends, and we were off to our destination. "So where are we going?"

"Gol Market, I know an ice cream shop there" Her reply after this was *truly* priceless for me, "Okay."

No, it's not the word, it's her 'expression'! I know it is lame but don't judge me, it was my first time on a date, well more like a hangout but, you get my point.

"So how is everything going with you? Many teachers say that you keep smirking in between classes?"

I immediately got lost in the question, or rather what caused that smile. Her sharp eyes, wavy medium length hair, her soft lips… all the features started clicking in my mind. "Hello? Lost somewhere?"

"Oh no nothing, well it's nothing special just, you know, something, perhaps someone caught my mind."

"Oh, Hah I know, is it a secret crush?" I gulped hard and in a stuttering voice tried to deny it, which clearly was not helping at all. "Yea-yea I know, usually people do this when they are lost in someone's memory."

Well, she wasn't exactly wrong though, I had a feeling she may not be as innocent as I thought. We approached a crossing, a four-lane crossing. She slowly started walking and I went after her and was hoping she would need my help, or she got in some trouble, and I'd save her.

Of course, not this is not Bollywood, we just safely crossed the road without any issue. "How far is it? Now I *really* need an ice cream in this heat."

"Just a few buildings away, you see that alley. There it is."

I am you.

We reached there after a 10-minute walk and I was able to see that she was a bit tired, I paid for both the ice creams, she took black current, and I took double vanilla-chocolate cone. We were walking under the shade of a building… she was focused on ice cream, and I was focused on her.

"So, what do you like to do in free time?" I asked her in an attempt to start a conversation… what she said next made no sense to me, "Nothing… I just lie on my bed or watch some TV, helping my mother or my annoying brother sometimes."

"Well, I don't have a sibling so I can't really relate" she replied with such interest after I said this, "It's good that you don't have a sibling, they are a real pain to handle… like help them with their homework, listen to everything they say or else they'll complain to your parents, and they'll *always* take their side and not yours."

I was genuinely shocked and was thinking if siblings are really this much pain in the ass… like I've seen my father with his brothers, my uncles and they bond like they've never been separated, I guess it's different for everyone.

"I wish I had a sister; it would've been fun to have one, fun to not be the only kid in the house."

What she said next destroyed my mind, "I can be your sister if you want" she said it with a smirk, but I can't tell how shocked I was, 'Vaishnavi, you told me she feels the same for me, what is this?'

"No! I mean not like you can't be but, I just, don't want it… just ignore it I am not getting any girl as my sister."

"Yea-yea sure…" she just continued with her ice cream without asking anything else because I was prepared with the answer long before we even bought ice cream.

It's fine she might be just stressed… today was a little harder than rest of the days, we had to stand in the auditorium for a speech by Mrs. Vyaas and that wasn't even a big thing, some people or should I say 'couple' were caught kissing near the metro station, the authorities handed them over to the school.

I am you.

Now it might sound ironic because we are roaming together but we are not a couple, this is not a date, and I don't think anyone restricts people of the opposite gender to be friends. Funny I was thinking of this because she asked me a question about the same topic.

"What do you think about what Mrs. Vyaas told us today, were the couple really guilty?"

I gave it a bit of thought and in a smooth flow kept saying what I thought of the situation, "Well, I believe that there's nothing wrong with it, until and unless it is done in a way it doesn't disturb your work… since teenagers are usually very curious about stuff, some people do it just because they can. Not only does it distract you from other things, but you also don't really form a connection with that person. I can't exactly say whether those two were right or wrong since I don't know what their connection was, but I say if you come into a relationship, be it in any age, take it responsibly, and if you genuinely believe you are not ready, don't do it… it's not a status symbol to have a partner, so just be rational"

Kartikeya Sharma.

Not only did I feel really smart after that, but I also believe I left a huge impression on her.

"Damn you are really an expert in this huh? Were you in a relationship before?" If I answer 'no' she can ask from, where do I have such an experience, or she can just compliment me. I cannot say yes but I can answer the question with a question. In an attempt to keep the conversation going, I answered by saying, "Do you think so?"

"Well, you don't seem like a guy who has been in relationship, but your big talks say it otherwise, I'll go with you were in a situationship."

She got it in the center, which wasn't what I expected, "Wrong, I never had a partner" I said confidently.

We reached to the school again and it was time for us to head homes, "Well it was nice hanging out with you Krish."

"Yea me too, it was a nice little break, hopefully we'll do it again sometime" While saying the last line, I don't know why but I felt like a certain uncertainty, like I

I am you.

was unsure whether what I said is what I mean… not giving anymore thought to it for now, we fist bumped and we started walking towards home.

On the way I was having a heavy clash in my mind, not exactly sure about what but something didn't feel right, like I was missing on something, or perhaps someone.

After coming home, I freshened up, sat on my table and as I was thinking of what homework to do, I realized I had none… I completed everything in school so all I had left to do was a bit of preparation for the exam and I'd be over for the weekend.

I opened my favorite subject, English and began revising the chapters and attempting some questions, in the middle of the session, I saw my sketch book opened on the table, not being able to resist, I threw the books and looked at the sketch, she was almost complete, I just had to draw what kind of clothes she would be wearing…

Suddenly I smelt something, no it was not the food but something which triggers all the dopamine in my tiny teenage brain, smell of wet dirt… and that indicates, "It's about to rain!"

I stood up and looked at my window, I saw droplets which were slowly increasing and increasing till all I could hear was the splash of rain drops. "Oh, boy let's have some fun."

I went to my balcony and saw the atmosphere all foggy, as if the render distance had been reduced. I quickly removed my jacket and even though it being the month of cold November, I planned to go outside. I came from a really sunny afternoon, and I met this beautiful weather.

"MOM I am going outside, I'll be back when the streetlights start glowing."

I took my go pro as well which I got last year and as I went out the gate… the water started spreading through all of my clothes and not even five seconds standing, I was soaking wet.

It's been a while I've been in rain, especially in November based on I live in North India, but it was a really nice and relaxing feeling. I slowly started walking

I am you.

around my area, enjoying the drops which felt like bullets on my face when I looked up in the sky.

"*This* is life" I said, and I really meant it, out of all the things that happened today, this was the best and even better than my hangout today.

"Let's turn this thing on" I started filming the surroundings, but I didn't really care for it to be a perfect footage… I was just enjoying what I was seeing…

"Oh my… now this will be fun" I saw a big puddle filled with water and dirt in the park. Whenever I see puddles of water, unless I am going to a wedding I am *bound* to jump in it, this moment was no different. I walked through the gate of the park and stood there looking at the puddle… I set up the go pro near the swing and then returned to my position.

I ran, ran as fast as I could, and I did what I haven't done in three months. I knee slide across the puddle, the water went splashing like a tsunami ahead of me.

Kartikeya Sharma.

"This, is what gives me happiness, other than homemade Dal Chawal or hanging out with my friends."

I sat there for a while just thinking about today... I gave a thought to today's hangout with Nandini, and I figured that she is quite different from me, like she doesn't like having siblings, she isn't really very smart in guessing that I have feelings for her which I clearly indicated her, I mean, I guess I didn't. I just asked her to ice cream and didn't make any effort to *flirt* with her.

Now I don't blame her, every person is *different,* and maybe that's the reason I was doubtful after the hang out. I think maybe my thinking about her being the perfect partner for me is a little off.

"What am I even doing? Since last year this is the first time, I had talked to her with full interest, or I should rather say alone."

The streetlights turned on and my time was over... I stood up, picked up my go pro and went to my house. It was around 7 p.m. when I reached home, dripping all the way till bathroom...

I am you.

When I turned on the shower, I made the worst
mistake, I turned the tap towards cold water and the
moment when it touched my cold skin, it was like
needles piercing my body… I hurriedly turned the tap to
other side and the only thing I was thinking at that time
was, "Oh for sake *please* turn hot FAST!"

I spent like half an hour in the bathroom because
I *love* a hot bath in the first place and second that I just
came after jumping in mud, so I had to wash everything
off…

Now here's a funny thing which I don't know if
it only happens to me or everyone, but I always get really
sleepy whenever I go out in the rain and then take a bath
after that. This time was no different, I came out of
bathroom and sat at dinner table, I tried to eat a bit less
because I was already feeling lazy, and I didn't want to
feel even more so when I am completing my sketch,
when the carbs start to break down in my body.

"Mom I'll be waking up late tonight, tomorrow is
Sunday and I've done all the studies after getting home."

I said this because I didn't want to wake up in the middle of the night and then sleep again, I just wanted to wake up late and then sleep in the morning till whenever I wanted.

"Oh Sure, just don't wake up too long so you don't stress yourself out in the morning, ok?"

That's exactly the answer what I wanted, I hoped she responded the same if I asked her to ask Nandini out, but who am I kidding, this is India., "Yea sure mom I'll sleep around 1:30 a.m. most probably before that."

She agreed with a nod while eating. I got excited, I will finally be able to complete the sketch and then talk to her all day.

That was the whole reason I was making her, to have someone to talk to who is just like me, and it was already effective, I talked to her two times but at that time she wasn't exactly like me since I didn't write the full personality of her, but now that I have, I can even talk to her in the middle of making her clothes.

Let's see where this rainy night takes me…

I am you.

Chapter 5

-Into the unknown

I got to my room, and instead of sitting at my table I sat on my bed because I wanted to just relax today. Instead of listening to music, I just listened to the heavy downpour while I turned on my nightlamp on my nightstand. I just wore a thin T-shirt and an oversized hoodie, I took the sketch book and sat on my bed, I took my extra pillow and put it behind my back and the comfort I got was far more superior than if I would've sat on my chair.

I stared at her for a while, thinking about what I should make her wear, "Formal? No, it'll not be so fun, then casual like T-shirt or hoodies and pajamas? Eh, not getting the vibe, then some armor. A metal suit with different colored clothes wrapped around it for design and a ponytail on her head, a giant axe, or a sword… no I'll have a sword, she is better with an axe.

Kartikeya Sharma.

What am I doing she's not a 14th century warrior, let me just make a simple lehenga, or kurta salwar… shit I am so bad in making decisions, and women's clothing, it's like asking a fish to fly.

Wait let me search what both look like, or especially which is better"

I opened my laptop and searched both… I first searched kurta salwar, and it looked *really* good but when I searched up a lehenga, OH MY GOD it looked SO gorgeous, I mean sure it was a formal dress after all but nothing like a suit blazer, it was beautiful but there was only one problem, it's only for special occasions, so I went for an easier option, Salwar Kameez…

I opened the photo on my laptop and started drawing it, it was 11:21 p.m. when I checked the time, I still had plenty of time to finish and to just admire her. I started making the layer of kameez first and slightly made the design on it, then I went for the dupatta and as

I am you.

I was making the salwar… my eyes started to get really heavy, "Oh no the rain fatigue is catching up on me"

I tried to open my eyes the best I could and just tried to finish as fast as I could but made sure I didn't mess it up.

I closed my eyes for a moment in hopes for a longer duration of focus, I know it makes no sense but it's better than having caffeine. So, I closed them for like *two seconds* and when I opened, I was not in my bedroom anymore… I was in a city in the middle of a HUGE terrain… filled with grass, forests and just highlands… when I looked up there wasn't a thing called "sky" I could see the whole space from below, the planets, stars, galaxies and *everything*.

It was *just* so beautiful I cannot describe, I had never seen such a thing, or dream I guess…I started walking around the city and all I could see were the students in my school. All were in their casual clothes… it was as if all of them had their own world, without parents, teachers, schools, taxes, government or anything else like that.

Kartikeya Sharma.

It was like a secret city of theirs where no one is bound by any sort of rules or regulations or anything. I was wandering around seeing all sorts of students… some hanging out with their girlfriends… who am I kidding almost everyone was on a date with their partners, I guess this is everyone's wish, to freely walk hand in hand with their partner.

"I wonder where Aditya and Nikhil are, surely, they won't be roaming with a girl, I started roaming around and honestly it was really nice, it was like two lane roads with buildings all over, kind of like a Minecraft village but highly developed. It would have taken me a long time to roam around the city with my legs…

I tried to find public transportation like bus or auto rickshaw, if they exist here or perhaps a friend who can give me a lift.

I am you.

I noticed there were no streetlamps whatsoever, the place was solely lit by the bright galaxy above me. The city was built on just terrain, there was short grass as soon as the foot path ended, and the houses and buildings just stood there like a Lego house in a park.

The place was absolutely amazing, I was starting to believe this was the best dream I've had… I walked around the small city and to be honest it was actually really small like it would've been like I think not more than 4-kilometer squares. I didn't find Aditya or Nikhil, but I found Raghav, one of my classmates.

He was looking in the bonnet of his car, and it was a Corolla, I mean, not a bad choice but I just saw an Aston Martin on my way here, "Hey Raghav!"

"Oh, hey Krishay, you found this place as well huh?" I mean he was saying as if this was their secret hideout, this was *my* dream.

"Yea why not now tell me where I will find Adit-no wait" I had a better idea, "Where's Nandini?"

I mean, this was my dream, why not take the chance? "Oh, sure she is probably hanging out near the mall I think, on the other side of the city, and I would happily take you there if you help me fix my car."

I was almost laughing to myself, "Ok you do know I can get there like in less than five minutes and second… how did you even manage to break down a Corolla?"

He was thinking forever and what finally came out of his mouth was the stupidest excuse I've ever heard, "I accidentally added coolant in place of engine oil."

I didn't say anything and just walked away, without looking at him, "I guess a Corolla *can* break down."

I kept walking towards the mall and on my way, I found many known people, I mean all of them were known, that's why they were in my dream. There was Rohit as well, that rotten to the core guy, I thought of having fun with him but no, I didn't know how long this dream would go so I ignored him.

I am you.

"There it is the mall" I slowly walked towards it and immediately burst into a laughter by reading 'Mall with Children.'

"They couldn't find a better name for it" I was still laughing, and many students were staring at me... I slowly started walking again while trying to control my laugh"

I was about to reach the mall when someone hugged me from behind with a high-pitched laugh, I immediately turned back, and it was Rupali and OH MY! She was wearing a full lehenga as if she was going to a wedding, HER OWN WEDDING!

Hii Krishay! So, you are here too huh? The next thing I noticed was surprising yet expected. She was trying to flirt with me! I kept staring at her and the fact that she was just *three* inches far from me, "You know Krishay if you keep looking at me like this, I might fall for you."

As soon as she said that she feels towards me, resting her hands on my chest and looking dead in my eyes, I was in sleep, but the heart rate was already past what it usually is in front of Nandini.

Kartikeya Sharma.

"Standing next to you makes my heart do weird things, care to explain?"

How did she know I was thinking about stuff related to heart!

"Rupali, uh take easy on yourself you should probably head home, or wherever you stay in this place."

"Krishay, you're really not making this easy for me. How am I supposed to focus on anything else when you look *this* good?"

She smirked and her finger ran down my chest.

I felt my soul LEAVING MY BODY.

We are in the MIDDLE of the ROAD! You are flirting with me in front of all these people! I tried this to let her go of me, none of the students cared about what was happening.

I tried to lift her hands and walk away, but it was my mistake, as I was turning back, she held my wrist, "Tell me, Krishay… do you have any idea how dangerously charming you are?" She tilted her head waiting for me to react.

60

I am you.

My reaction? I was TOMATO RED, and she wanted to get my reaction! Her scent was a mix of floral perfume and red bull. Her pupils were dilated and her grip on my shoulders was growing loose every second.

Her smirk faded away, her eyes began to close as she leaned in for a kiss, I started to think of any solution other than punching her which was the first thing that came in my mind, she almost succeeded if it were not for my baggy hoodie, I slipped off it from beneath and ran like a turkey.

"HEY! Come back!" she called for me like two seconds later.

Nope. Nope. NOPE.

Nandini can kill herself for all I care—I am NOT going back. I sprinted like my life depended on it, and thankfully, the town's border wasn't far. The mall was right at the edge, and within moments, I was out.

As I stepped beyond the last building, the city's hum faded behind me, continuing with an endless terrain. The ground was uneven—some patches were covered in soft, short grass that shimmered like tiny stars under the celestial glow, while others were barren, dry dirt. The sky… well… There was no 'sky' at all, an ocean of galaxies, spirals of blue and violet, golden nebulae glowing like Diwali lights. The stars were not just tiny dots of light; they were enormous. Their glow bathed the land in a dreamlike silver hue, making every shadow stretch unnaturally long.

I felt as if I was in heaven, there was nothing but the terrain with no trees and the enormous space above me. There was no need for any light. Everything was just as clear as on a sunny day but far more enchanted.

The wind started to blow softly, it swayed my hair and the fabric of my thin T-shirt, the grass was moving as if responding to each movement of mine, as if it were alive. Above, the galaxies slowly spun, their light shifting in color like an aurora reaching across infinity. There was no end and the only thing limiting my sight was the horizon.

I am you.

"This is a dream, but I feel like I am actually feeling all this. This. Is. Marvellous!"

It was silent but not the kind I feel when I am alone, it felt like the world was listening to me. A low hum would flow through the air, like a cosmic whisper, it felt like the universe was itself speaking.

It started to shower crystal clear water, it was not rain, the small water drops which felt like the sky exhaled mist woven liquid glass. It was touching my skin like a soft hand and then vanishing just like that.

"Oh boy, this is going to be fun…"

Chapter 6

-Have we met?

After some time, I started walking, but *not* towards the town, I don't care about Nandini as of now, she has been in my dreams many a times, but this is special. I was starting to feel a bit cold… stupid Rupali made me lose my hoodie, I started searching for something; perhaps maybe another town or something.

It was a lucid dream, but I wasn't completely able to control it at that time, I was just aware I was in a beautiful surreal dream. Slowly that also started to wither, and I could feel that slowly I was gaining the ability to control the dream completely.

I climbed a highland and at a distance ahead I found a small village, it had just eight houses by count and a small pond.

"I may find something useful in there."

I slowly walked down the highland and upon closer inspection there was no one there, just small

I am you.

houses fully furnished. I tried to open a door, and it was locked, I tried the window, but it was not glass, it was trapdoor.

"If this is my dream, how about I try something; to open this door"

I tried to focus, like Dr. Strange, for a while I was standing there like idiots, I tried harder but then I realized,

I didn't know what I was hoping for.

I tried to formulate a key for the door; what I've learned from my past lucid dreams is that if you intentionally try to close your eyes and then open them, you just wake up, so that's what I was *not* going to do.

I just looked up in the beautiful sky and then looked down and VOILA! I had a key in my hand!

click it opened the door.

I entered the house in the *utmost* hope I'd find a jacket… it was after finding a trench coat in the wardrobe that I realized I could've summoned my own clothes.

Kartikeya Sharma.

"I should not do it often or else I'd put myself to risk of waking up, I don't want that, in fact I'd be happy to live here forever"

I got out of the house in my trench coat and a navy-blue pair of jeans, my favorite color for jeans and flat shoes…

"Whoever owns this house has a dope wardrobe."

Now that I was free from the cold, I decided to go near the pond and what awaited me there, I never gave it a thought. I slowly moved towards the magical blue pond with enchanted plants growing in it. It was pure blue lagoon, and it reflected the starry night.

As I went closer, I another small village like this one… I decided to see what magic that cluster of nine houses possessed…

I ran across the magical meadows and as soon as I reached there, I saw a person in a distance, I reduced my pace and slowly started approaching her, "Another

I am you.

person outside the city? Let's see who this is... looks like a woman to me"

I slowly started to believe it was Nandini, that belief turned to hope as she also started to walk towards me. Her face was dark, covered in the shadows of the houses.

The shadow left her face and as soon as her face was revealed by the light, I stood there absolutely blank. My face turned pale, my spine ran with a cold shiver... the person, the girl in front of me; same height as me, figure tall and poised, I turned to finally see her face-

And my breath hitched

She was *just* like me, her cascade fell to her shoulders, she had sharp brown eyes and heart shaped lips.

She looked like a reflection of myself, nothing like any person I've met in real life.

God

She looked at me just like I was inspecting, perhaps admiring her, we both tilted our heads a bit at

the same time and squinched out eyes. My surprise slowly started to let go of me as I realized I was inside my unconscious mind and a girl just tried to kiss me here.

"You look so much like me, probably the result of my self-obsession" I said it as I was processing what she was.

She did not like it…

"Hey-hey mister I look like you? You look like me" she stepped closer to me, her voice sharp. She held my face, turning it left then right, inspecting me like her unfinished work "You look like that drawing I was making" her whisper shook my insides, "My drawing"

I remembered, **yes**; she did look like my sketch.

"What do you mean your drawing, you look like my drawing… well just that you are wearing some kajal, and uh your hairs are open… what else you are wearing a hoodie and sweatpants"

I slowly started to list the differences between her and my sketch which I wasn't completely able to

I am you.

imagine, I forgot what name I gave to her or how exactly her face looked.

Only vague memories of her lingered in my mind-

"Ouch!"

She pushed me!

"The hell you are talking about, you are a little piece of imagination in my unconscious mind"

I became furious, "Excuse me, **I** am the imagination here?"

"That's exactly what I said fart for brains, but I guess you don't *have* a brain… because you are **in** my brain"

"Looks like a background character got TOO self-aware. Why did you come here, someone tried to kiss you when you were finding your crush huh?" her eyes widened from shock as if I shot her with a .45 caliber.

She approached closer to me; I stood my ground because I knew she wasn't going to do anything like Rupali… which I was not sure of actually.

"How…" she paused, "do you know this?"

I got confused, "How I know what? Wait, my guess was true?"

She stepped back in disbelief,

Who are you?

I came to realize, my guess was true; But how? This just happened to me a few minutes ago.

I clenched my fists and took and pulled up my stance.

A chill ran down my spine

She started pulling her stance *exactly* the moment I raised my arms; our stance was *exactly* the same. We slowly lifted our hands near our faces and spread our legs, "I won't get sad…"

"Making a little piece of my dream feel pain" she completed my sentence; I was scared but I wanted to know who she really was.

"Let's see, if she knows everything I do, she'll also know I never attack first"

I am you.

I will attack first.

I lunged forward with a right jab; she **dodged**…
and not with a didge, she just stepped back like she knew
I was going for her face. Before I could react, she
countered with a left hook going for my ribs, I twisted
my body right in time, barely escaping the hit.

We both looked at each other, eyes locked,
stance unshaken thinking only *one* thing.

How is this possible?

She stepped forward, delivering a low kick to my
leg, I moved to block; she **faked** it. Her attack came
from above, her elbow coming for my temple.

I barely ducked, feeling the presence of her arm above
my head, she was fast; though it's my turn now.

I pushed her, turning for a powerful back kick
but she held it! She held it with both hands and threw me
towards a house.

I somehow managed to land that flip, I looked at
her eyes, it contained confidence as well as tension. We

both ran towards each other, I knew she'd go for an aerial kick.

I. Was. Right.

She tuned her head down and jumped into a front flip with her legs straight, aiming for my body. She landed and I was already behind her, I went for a side kick aimed at her back.

She twisted.

She picked up a BIG, LONG cue lying in a box on ground. "Hey-hey, that's too much, that's not fair"

"Shut your mouth up, I won't feel bad hitting a person *in* my dream"

I ran, but the strange thing was, as soon as I put my foot down, the ground seemed to shake under it. It was as if my foot was as heavy as a truck.

I ran and what did I know… I was clocking around 100 km/h with no efforts or such, "This is CRAZY!" I laughed at my own speed even though I have jumped like a ten-meter gap or have lifted a whole mountain like Lord Krishna… I have even flown once

I am you.

like Cyborg, trying to catch spiderman who stole a big crystal from Jinx.

This just felt *so* surreal and *so* awesome, I was ACTUALLY feeling like I was going a hundred kilometers per hour.

I turned back and she was behind me, trying to catch up on me.

She still had the cue.

If I slow down even a little bit, I am pretty sure that cue is going straight up my ass, and she'll crucify me right here in the middle of this terrain. I wonder if I'll wake up after that, but I am not taking any chances.

I saw another abandoned village in a distance, but this time the houses weren't maintained at all, they were all broken and dirty.

"I'll have to go there if I want my survival chances to exceed the chances that Nandini will be my wife!"

Chapter 7

-I am you

I ran towards the village as fast as I could; I saw a problem I had to overcome, if I didn't slow down, I'd not be able to stop myself, and if I stopped, she was right behind me with the cue.

"I don't have much time I **have** to do something right now" I tried to go my way around the village and what I saw next blew my mind, across the village I saw a MASSIVE, shining blue seashore, whose crystal-clear blue lagoon water stretched as far as the eye can see, in this case the horizon.

Not only it looked **absolutely unreal**, which it was… I saw a plan, "If I just go right into the water, she'd also slow down along with me. Wait, this is a dream, **what if she just jumped from the shore** and **burst my body right in the water!"**

The village was already here, I finally thought about what to do and it wasn't the best plan, but it did

I am you.

work for me; I just broke through the wall of a house. I was pretty sure my shoulder was dislocated, which was still a surprise considering I should've just evaporated and destroyed the entire village as a result of more than 200 Gigajoules which **should** have been released when I smashed through the building.

Just as I settled on the fact that I was alive, she flew right through the hole I had just created in the wall of this small dirty house and smashed right through the other wall which was still intact.

I looked at her, she looked at me, "Yes!" I said it under my breath. "Let me guess, you are celebrating because my cue broke into literal **atoms?**"

Yup she knew it.

Dust was just starting to settle when the wooden pillars started to creak and eventually one of them cracked; the walls started to collapse, the roof was about to fall and the only thing we could do was stare at each other's face which clearly said,

"Yea we are screwed"

The house finally collapsed, and the destruction took around a minute to completely stop. The debris and dust were all around the place and I was under them, completely covered with it. I tried to remove the debris, but my left hand was already injured enough and now it was crushed under it.

"Is this really a dream… because if this didn't wake me up, I don't know what will."

I tried to remove the big piece of roof covering my face, after some efforts I was able to see the celestial abyss.

After a while I heard some sound, the sound of things moving, I tried to see what made the noise. All I could see was that some pieces of house were moving, then my mind was again in place,

That girl.

She must've also been crushed; little did I know she had already stood up and was coming to help me. Without any words of teasing or hatred, she immediately started

I am you.

removing the debris on me. My body was finally exposed and was covered in dust but absolutely *no* injuries.

My eyes studied her body, she didn't have a single scratch as well. She helped me get up and by the time we got out of that mess, we didn't speak a single word. We both sat against the wall of another house. We both were breathing heavily, and I was holding my shoulder, "Why am I caring about *your* shoulder, you're in my dream, I'll wake up and you'll be just gone"

My thoughts got in place, she was right, not about the fact that I was her dream character, but that if I wake up this won't matter. I tried to move my arm and as soon as it responded normally, my eyes widened with shock.

It was absolutely fine, as if no injury had been made, the dislocated shoulder and fractured humerus just left like went away like students during lunch break. I looked at her in shock, she was looking at my arm.

"I am confused, if this is my dream, you shouldn't be knowing it is a dream, and if you do, these weird things shouldn't be happening to you" her words made total sense. I had been thinking about this when I saw her running at my pace, "You're so right, I have no idea what is happening"

We both kept sitting giving this topic a deep thought, we looked at each other, my reflection was not only in her eyes but in her whole face. We stood up to test if what she just said was really true.

We tried to summon a hot wheel and to our surprise, not only did it work, but we also summoned the *same* hot wheel, a Need for Speed Most Wanted based BMW M3 GTR.

Impossible.

We were completely dazzled, we both reached out our hands, focused for like two seconds and I had a big sharp sword in my hand with a leather strap at the end of handle, glowing with blue lines like the water bodies here. I looked at her, she had a Labrys in her hand, a two headed axe with blue line like in my sword with the same leather strap on the end of handle.

We both dropped our weapons on the ground in fear and extreme disbelief. I tried to jump, and on my second jump I was on the top of the house. She followed

I am you.

me and now we were in a four-meter-tall building with
just a single jump. We looked at each other, I
remembered she dodged my every move and so did I.

In one moment, we both said to each other, "Hit
me"

We extended our hands towards the ground
where our weapons were lying, they came flying towards
us in not less than a single second.

In a single swift we both turned, attacking the
other with a powerful slash and in one moment they
both clashed with an enchanted sound, I swayed my
sword in circles, and she kept backing up. She did a *really*
high aerial cartwheel and landed behind me.

She slashed her axe trying to cut me in half, I
held my sword's handle with one hand and the blade
with another and blocked her axe right before hitting my
body. I felt something weird, "I know everything she is
going to do, but so does she"

We kept slashing our weapons to each other, the
symphony of steel and sparks filled the air with the
enchanted tone they produced as they sliced the thin air.

I threw the sword at her which was exactly what she did with her axe.

OH SHIT!

I am no gymnast, but I performed a straight leg aerial backflip and the same is said for her. The weapons went out of sight in no time across the vast dreamland.

We landed on our feet and as I tried to punch her, she grabbed my hand. I extended my other arm for my sword, and she did the same for her axe.

HMMM, with a soothing enchanted sound they came to our hands, in a big slash I tried to attack her, she jumped back immediately but immediately lost her balance to the edge of building and she fell down.

I stood there like an idiot, didn't know what to do. I lowered my sword and stepped closer to the edge. She was lying on a big stack of hay.

No explanation, no proper reason, we both burst into loud laughs. We slowly stopped and I looked at her in pity, "You are definitely an NPC if not a part of my dream"

I am you.

She was still trying to stop her laughing but then it suddenly stopped followed by a sudden silence in her tone. She was staring at me, "Uh hello what happened?" She pointed at me, or that's what I thought, I turned back and looked up and it was as if my eyes would fall into my eye socket.

Suspended in the endless abyss were two celestial bodies- no, universes… huge and radiant, mirroring each other. Their luminous edges gave an enchanted and ethereal glow, aligned in perfect parallel. They weren't just reflections; they existed side by side defying every logic and every rule of physics.

An **Event Horizon**… of two aligned. Symmetrical. Echoing. **Parallel Universes**

My eyes were too small to accommodate such sight, it was a never seen, never imagined phenomenon. I heard some rustles behind me… she stood up, but her eyes were fixed on this amazing and *stunning* scene.

Kartikeya Sharma.

I jumped down and we both kept looking at this scene. I looked at her. She looked at me and in one tone we asked, "What's your name?"

It was all beginning to make sense, our similar thoughts, same thinking, intermixing looks,

Krishay Sharma… Kritika Sharma

Our eyes widened as we heard the names. We kept looking at our reflections in the other's eyes, or perhaps the whole face, "You know what this means right?" she asked me in amusement.

"Totally"

We stepped closer till we were no more than just a finger space apart, our eyes locked with each other's.

With an amused and carefree smile, our eyes started to fill with water, we cupped each other's cheeks, tilted our heads and in unison we whispered with tears running down our cheeks,

I am you.

82

Chapter 8

-Echoes of me

She… was me, and I was her. We were one person, from different worlds or what we call 'Parallel Universes'

We were fighting ourselves all this time, it all makes sense now; we knew exactly what the other had in mind and knew exactly what the other would do. My mind was an ocean of shock and unbelievable happiness.

"I found a person *just* like me" she completed my sentence, "I found a person who is literally me"

We stood there as if the time was frozen, our minds were processing the truth which had revealed before us. Her face was covered in the surreal glow by the universes, I think it was the same for me. Without thinking, without any hesitation, we moved at the same time.

We reached out our arms and before we knew it, we were holding each other tightly. It didn't feel like just a simple hug, it was as if I was holding a lost piece of my own soul, a part of me which I never had but always existed. I felt her heartbeat against mine perfectly synced, as if we shared the same pulse across dimensions.

She buried her face in my shoulder and for the first time, the tears flowing down my cheeks didn't contain sadness but pure and unfiltered joy, "I thought I was alone" I whispered under my voice

"Me too, but I guess we are finally not, we are not alone anymore"

We stood there for what felt like an eternity, completely lost in each other's warmth. The world around us, the horizon, the houses, the far stretched dreamland, none of it mattered… we were too lost in each other to see anything else around us.

We had found each other

We weren't just two people from different worlds…

We were one.

She pulled a little back, her hands were still on my shoulders, her tears containing the same emotions I was feeling, "So… what now?" she asked while wiping

I am you.

her tears. "I don't know, after seeing two dimensions interconnecting, I don't think I have anything to see now.

She gave a slight laugh, "Wait, you said you also ran from a town where someone was trying to kiss you, this is *exactly* what happened to me!" she looked at me in amusement but soon it turned into an obvious face, "Well I am not surprised now that I know this dream belongs to *both* of us."

I wanted to see how her town looked like, "Why not we go to your town?"

She said with an expression which clearly showed she was expecting me to say this, "I wanted to see your town first"

Now this was a bit of confusion… I didn't want to go back to my town, but now I know she also didn't want to go there first. I knew she was also thinking about that and in one unison we both said,

"LET'S RACE"

We both stood up in on a little highland near the village… far away we could see many small groups of houses, and some were big enough to be called villages.

"Let's race till the village with that small pond. It's near the village I met you and I got this junky Tench coat from one of its houses"

"Which type of cars should we take? Sports, hyper or old time?"

I smirked at her and she reciprocated… "We both know what we want" We both ran down the highland and focused on the ground and the next moment there was a Lamborghini Sesto Elemento in front of my eyes… gleaming in the radiant glow of the world.

Beautiful.

I was admiring it from all sides while Kritika was thinking about what car she should pick.

She finally decided and within a moment there was a white Porsche 918 Spyder in stunning carbon fiber spoiler, "This is gorgeous, *and* it has no roof."

"I am supposing you know what to do before we race right?" Yup I knew it… a **rev battle**. I hopped in

I am you.

my car and started it at once, the V10 was absolutely **brutal**. Kritika had to cover her ears it was so loud, "THAT's how I like it!" it ended with some pops and bangs, I lifted my foot off the throttle,

"Your turn sweet pea!" I shouted with full strength because there was a fire breathing 5.2-liter beast of an engine right behind me.

She quickly hopped in the Spyder and when she gave the throttle, we both realized it was a twin turbo hybrid, so it didn't sound as raw as we thought, "Hey Crybaby! You should've thought about that before you picked that car."

"The sound doesn't matter wet underpants, the performance does… I am surprised that you, or in this case *I* didn't think of this."

I buckled up and shifted into first gear… she did the same except she had launch control, "Let's do this."

After three seconds we landed full throttle,

"This is crazy!"

My car was so loud I couldn't hear the 918 which was a bit ahead of me due to the control…

Kartikeya Sharma.

"I think sports cars on dirt and grass terrain was a bad idea… not like I care about the cars, but this suspension has no comfort or anything which can save my butt from these small bumps."

I noticed I was barely going above a hundred kilometers, "Screw my ass let's go" I stepped down on the gas pedal and the car was just gone, it's screaming was so loud I couldn't hear my own voice of excitement.

I watched in the rear-view mirror, Kritika was catching up to me, "Of course she also stepped down on the gas" I was at 180 kilometers per hour, and it was increasing. I looked to my left and her car was right beside me, she flipped me off and her car slowly started to gain the lead… "Not on my watch"

I risked it and tapped my car's bonnet to her rear fender, her car was out of control, "Here's my chance" I turned to the right and with full pace took the lead, before I knew it, I jumped off a raised land in front of me.

My car was in the air.

I landed and I knew I was defeated now.

I am you.

The car hit the ground with an impact which I could feel right through my spine, the car kept jumping and twitching around, unable to stabilize.

"Just don't roll over. Don't roll over. For God's sake **don't roll over!"**

I saw her behind me, she was catching up fast. I looked back and there it was, The Village! "What is happening?" I tried to turn the wheel, but it didn't budge…

I broke the wheel axle.

I was in too much tension to focus and try to fix the car… I pushed the throttle harder and after just a few moments, I heard some cracking and screeching sound, "No. No. No please don't say the underbody is destroyed."

It wasn't coming from my car.

I looked behind, her 918 had a broken splitter which was stuck under her car making her slow. "This is my chance."

Kartikeya Sharma.

With all my strength I *finally* reached the town, or that was what I thought, my axle bent completely causing an immediate stop to the car,

"What the… NO I am barely *fifty* meters away!" She won the race, and I didn't even come second, or last in this case… I wasn't even able to complete the race. I saw her stepped out of her car in anger.

"Yup I am getting my ass whooped… verbally though she can't hurt me" I unbuckled and stepped out of the car, my neck and spine needed serious therapy.

"Ughh Sharma, you have some **serious** explaining to do **right** now!" she was obviously talking about me trying to sabotage her. "I know. I know I tried to push you and all but there weren't any rules, ok?"

Her tone didn't change, "Do you really think I care about that? I won and that's what really matters."

"Oh, right then she's definitely mad about what I have done to this Lamborghini" I thought with an unbothered face.

I am you.

"What have you done to this sweet and stunning ride!" told you. I looked back and I was shocked myself, its headlights were broken, its front right wheel turned ninety degrees to the right, and it was covered in dents.

"It's a dream, yet I feel bad for this rare piece of art machine to be broken like so" she agreed with a nod and slight hum. "So, since I won the race, we are going to your town first."

I remembered the bet and took a deep breath of sigh, "Let's go it's about half a kilometer from here that side" I pointed my finger at the direction of the town which wasn't properly visible because of the village near the pond.

"Let's go on this point" her way of speaking and phrases were the same as mine.

I prefer to walk and talk on the way more than go in a vehicle and if course she does as well. "Let's play a game" I suggested.

"We will guess about each other's life, right?" That's exactly what I had in mind, instead of agreeing to it, I just started 'guessing.'

"So according to me you are a single child and live in North India" without giving any thought she answered in a silent hum, she asked immediately, "You have a crush on a girl with whom you went on a date before you entered this dream"

Although I knew she was me, every line which came out of her mouth… passing through her beautiful lips took me by a little surprise. Yup I was focusing on her face than her words. I took advantage of the fact she knows everything about me,

"So, I say you were making a sketch named 'Krishay' then slept and came into this dream, you met me and started to fall for me." My cheeks immediately turned red but as expected, her cheeks were red as well… we kept looking at each other for a while and in a really low whisper, she looked down and said, "True".

I was having trouble looking at her as she was having, "I say you're having an adrenaline rush just like me."

I am you.

She made me put a little smile on my face,

"You're right"

Chapter 9

-One romantic night

After a while the people or 'students' came to our sight as we approached closer and closer to the town… the same town from where I ran away.

"I need to make sure I don't come in sight of that evil… EVIL Rupali" She looked at me in confusion, "Rupali? She was the one who was trying to kiss you?" I agreed with a little uncertainty in my tone.

"It was Rajesh for me, he was acting all flirty and *daring* which is absolutely opposite of what he is in real world… he'd usually act all shy around me and the only daring thing he did for me is to ask me for ice cream"

This is *exactly* what happened to me… her life was really just my life… with I guess all the genders are changed. We entered the town, and it was exactly like I left it, I don't know how much time ago the time is going crazy here… or maybe there is no such thing as 'time'.

I am you.

She was looking around in awe and I was making sure Rupali didn't see me. "I have probably never met these people, but they look exactly like the people in my world" she paused and stopped, "Wha- What happened? Did you see Rupali somewhere?" I hid my face in my coat

"Is that your crush? Over there by the fire hydrant" she pointed at her, "Yup she is it, Nandini. I wasn't able to find her in the first place but… I suppose you already know that"

She observed her carefully and whispered under her breath, "Didn't think he would look this good as a girl"

"What? I didn't hear it can you say that again" she got flustered and immediately blinked her sight off Nandini, "Oh uh nothing… nothing really"

We kept walking forward to see what else was there, we planned to have fun with some people I or **we** hated like Rohit for example, and whatever he is called in her world. We decided to go to the mall because it was the biggest building of all the buildings.

Kartikeya Sharma.

"This is so damn beautiful!" her eyes were fixed on all the big bright chandeliers and the decorations. It was truly magnificent.

Although there was nothing special which we didn't see in a regular mall, and we weren't there just to eat KFC or play in the arcade. So, we just went to the little shops where they sell all kinds of small, cute stuff…

Money wasn't an issue; all we needed was something we could enjoy with. We went to a shop with collectibles and artifacts and none of them could draw our interest, we weren't the most interested in history. We were roaming around, having fun, joking around.

Suddenly I saw a person turning on a romantic song from a famous Bollywood movie. All the people in that area were looking at us while we were jumping and dancing around holding hands, we kept moving and I saw a big white lotus in a vase… I picked it up, did an effortless turn on the beat, stood right in front of her face…

We were still moving, or I should say oscillating on our place, I slid the flower in her hair and rested it

I am you.

above her ear. She smiled with a look which said, "Oh so you **ARE** doing it huh?"

Her eyes were wide, admiring my face, our eyes filled with the reflection of one another, her smile screamed shyness but also said the message of "I don't want this to end" My cheeks then ears started to burn, my abdomen was filled with unstable fluids… all I could see was her eyes, and my own reflection.

I was in love with myself.

Her eyes fall down to my lips and so did mine, I could feel her warm breath against my skin… our lips were almost about to press against each other… as soon as they came less than a single centimeter close, our body froze in the moment.

In a sudden moment we both opened our eyes and pulled back, our faces were wine like red, we were breathing heavily as we looked at each other with surprise. The claps, applauses, hooting and whistles were all over the place…

We both had a weird laugh and an expression on our faces which clearly asked for explanations about,

Kartikeya Sharma.

"What the hell just happened!?"

We looked around, everybody was still shouting and clapping as if we did something *really* big, not going to lie, we were actually about to, "I think we should run" I suggested, and then ran away, pushing across the crowd. I looked behind and she was following me.

The escalators were full of people, "Oh I always wanted to do this" I ran and with a Kong vault, followed by a front flip I jumped from the first floor to the ground floor. I looked back and she just did a side flip over the railing and came down. We were jogging side by side.

"Why were we about to do that?" she asked, "You already know I don't have a clear answer other than I never felt anything like this with anyone else."

She was taking deep breaths as if she is going to give the entrance for MIT, "Yea, I feel the same actually… I mean you would know, of course."

She gave out a laugh, "Shit this is so crazy I *still* can't believe it… I mean this whole dream and you and

I am you.

the thing which just happened above." By this time we were outside the mall.

We saw a locked house in a distance, I looked around and found a big crowbar. I broke the lock which I could do with my 'special powers' We both went inside, locked the door, closed the curtains and lay flat on the bed. We were breathing hard with all that dancing, running and jumping from the floor.

We both were confused about what just happened in the mall, we knew why we did it, but it was still a weird feeling. "I am sort of glad we didn't do it, not in a place like that."

She immediately turned her head towards me, "*Exactly*, I don't want it to happen among SO many people"

"Yea specially when these are the people who are *in* my school… I want to have my first… ahem" I got goosebumps with the next word, "kiss… to be somewhere nice, like in a park during night, walking with my partner" she cut my sentence immediately, "By partner you mean me, right?"

Kartikeya Sharma.

We both chuckled and with a spill of nervousness in my tone, I agreed like I was a little kid asking for a toy. She smiled and her face was now relaxed in the cozy bed, staring up the ceiling, "Me too".

After a while of rest, I was starting to feel a bit hungry, "Damn we could be hungry in a dream? I guess we should've stopped at KFC in the mall" She got up excitedly to check the fridge… I followed her and we found *absolutely* nothing. I guess we are **still** in India, we don't keep any food in the fridge just like that.

"Shouldn't we able to just, you know **spawn** the food?" Great idea. I stretched my hand and looked up and tried to imagine or think or wish or whatever this weird wish making is called but when I looked down, I had a twelve-piece fried chicken bucket.

"Let's party partner" she excitedly opened the drawer and took out two large plates. "I think there is some soft drinks in the cooler beside the fridge" I said after putting the bucket on the dining table.

"Are we ready?" She put down the plates and soda, "No wait we don't have the sauce." We both looked at each other.

I am you.

"Mustard?"

"Mustard" We got five mustard dips, and we sat to jump into the heaven which was in front of us. "I haven't eaten chicken in like a month" of course it was the same for me. We finished the bucket in less than fifteen minutes.

There were food crumbs and dips all over the table, our faces were all messed up, and our stomachs were never this fuller, it was like we'd eaten a whole week's ration. Just six pieces each did *this* to us, we really needed to increase our intake capacity.

"**One** of the best meals of this month for sure" We washed up and stood in the living room, and I mean it. We were just standing and looking into each other's eyes saying **absolutely** nothing.

We held each other's hands, together we both asked, "What to do now?" We both pretended to think with a 'hum' which also came out at the same time for both. "Let's get into a fight, and **win** it"

She continued my idea, "A fight with Scorpion gang, we hate it so much I always wanted someone of that gang to pick a fight with me, swear on my mother I would've punched their ego out of their soul."

"Although I suppose those are girls for you, here these are boys, I suppose stronger…" I knew we weren't backing down, but I wanted to see her reaction, "You wanted to see my reaction, didn't you?"

"You got me… let's go" we opened the door and looked for the gang, "Hey excuse me, do you know where Scorpion gang is right now?" I asked a girl on the street, we found out they were by the garages, resting on their vehicles. I imagined they had black trucks, green scorpion livery and spikes on bumpers.

"We ran through the busy streets and alleyways to their garage"

It was a gas station with a garage for three cars and the shop, or what they call their office' in these situations.

We smirked at each other and started walking in full confidence towards them…

They all were around their vehicles, which were two monster trucks and one pickup truck, some cleaning their vehicles, some sleeping on them and some just hanging out. They wore white T-Shirts with *Scorpio* printed on them and a black sleeveless jacket.

We stood in front of them about two car-lengths away. "HEY! What are you doing here? I warn you we don't let someone go without a broken bone or two if they mess with us" That was Ranveer, the leader… he cracked his knuckles as he stepped down from the truck and started walking towards us.

We looked at each other and then Ranveer… I changed my trench coat with a thin leather jacket, and my lowers to a pair of jeans. Kritika chose a light red parka with fur on the hoodie with a similar pair of jeans to mine.

Strangely, no one reacted to our superhero like outfit change- like it was a daily thing for them. They picked up bats, hockey sticks, metal rods, crowbars and everything they could use to beat up our asses.

"We won't use any weapons… it won't be fun" I said.

Kartikeya Sharma.

Some of them already didn't have anything to attack with. Some of them came out of the shop… they were not their gang members but their friends, both here and in real life… they were just under twenty people.

"Shall we start with a fancy dialog?" I asked her with excitement, I never got to use this dialog in real life.

"It's not something you ask Krish… I'll go after you" I looked at them and with a confident smile and I started speaking.

"You all are not even twenty in number…" she continued, "You don't have any idea how to fight in an arena…" I stepped forward and added, "Whoever seeks survival of his own shall leave this area right now" she stepped forward as well, "In a few moments this place will have a dance of death!"

"Now here, it will not be the beg of your mercy, but only your screams that will be heard!"

We both said in a hard, intimidating voice while snapping our fingers in sync… The leader let out a small chuckle and started moving forward. On the right moment I grabbed her hands, she grabbed mine and I

I am you.

spun her in the air and hit Ranveer with her legs… he flew away five tiles far to our right. I slowly put her on the ground as we saw everyone just running towards us.

One by one I tackled everyone, only a jab on the face to knock the first guy out and grabbed another in a wrist lock and kicked his ribs. Meanwhile Kritika was just enjoying the show… All I needed sometimes was an elbow punch to the face or neck and there they were lying on the ground.

I ran off to catch my breath and take in the sight… they were coming for me; I ran straight at them and with an aerial side kick right to the chest of the guy in front… the group began to fall like dominoes. I ran and jumped above them, using what we call the 'Dream Powers'

There were people looking at this very scene near the station and some from the roofs of other buildings,

"We are giving free entertainment to people without charging taxes, how nice of us"

Kartikeya Sharma.

"That was really rough" she said to me when I approached her, I clapped on her hands, signaling it's her shift now, she walked towards them and only used kicks… her kicking locus was just perfect… she was all spinning like a Kathak dancer, her shoulder length hair whipped like fluids on steroids

On of them hit her in the chest with a crowbar, she fell on the ground, gasping her pain, I ran towards him and delivered a strong uppercut to his chinless face. I helped her stand up and after a while her pain vanished.

Almost everyone was down except a few who were planning to take us down.

"This was really fun" she said in her exhausted but excited voice… her hairs were all messed up and all over her face, I just kept looking at her face and after a while we both found ourselves admiring each other in the middle of the station.

I brushed the hair strands with my hand off her face and she brushed the dust off my shoulders. We smiled at each other when we heard a scream from our right.

I am you.

One of the guys was charging towards us with a metal rod, I don't know what his plan was, but he struck the ground between us, we took a step back and grabbed his collars from both sides.

"You shouldn't shout before you attack" we both said it together, made him stand on his feet and…

Let's just say we broke his nose because I don't know what else in his skull got damaged by the fists of two people.

Or in this case just one person…

"We… did it" I said it but immediately looked at her, "Nope…" we said together.

I did it.

We looked at the place… after *such* a long time we fought like this… although maybe it's because we couldn't die there… and there were no legal bounds, or that's what I thought, I never saw any police till now.

"This felt really good Krishay…" I looked at her, we were once again lost in each other's eyes… "This is my favorite moment between us" I whispered to her.

Kartikeya Sharma.

She stepped closer to me, "Same for me" she rested her arms on my shoulders and locking them behind my neck.

"Now, Ms. Sharma… time to go see your side of the town." I wanted to see how my people look like as opposite gender.

"What do you say Mr. Sharma? How shall we go there?" I pretended to give it a deep thought, "How far is it exactly?"

"About five kilometers from here, can be more… why?" I gave it a thought and gave her a little smirk. "Follow me."

And *just* like that we were flying sky high in a Sukhoi SU-34 fighter jet with 'my little pony' livery all over it, because we both liked it very much, Fluttershy for the **win!**

I am you.

Chapter 10

-Where dreams get wings

She was flying it, and we were about fifteen seconds away from pressing the ejector seat button. I was lost in my own thoughts; something didn't give me a good feeling.

I looked at the Event Horizon to my left, it was a little out of place, like it wasn't how it was when we first saw it, the positions were a bit different, perhaps changed. I looked at her… she was unconcerned about the change I noticed.

"Oh right… this is just a dream. No matter how much I get attached, it'll fade away like all the others. Who knows if I'll ever see her again?" this thought left me at unease for the rest of the flight… I'm sure she isn't thinking *this*, she's flying such a powerful machine.

In the middle of my thinking session, Suddenly, a shock jolted us and the next thing I knew, we were launched into the sky with our seats. We were around

15,000 feet in air… both of us separated from our seats and were gliding through the thin wind.

"We should've worn a helmet; my eyes are burning like HELL!" I shouted with the top of my strength… and after realizing she can't hear me; I just used the hand signals.

"Just spawn it dumb ass!" Oh, yea I didn't think of that… in the next two seconds I had a helmet with a big visor. I looked at her and she did the same. **"Do you have an intercom?"**

I asked her with hand signs and the next thing I knew was her little broken voice in my helmet, "Did you try to talk in your helmet even once?"

Yup we had it… We started to see her town, it was small as a little LEGO city from up here. After a while I tried to control my flight; I failed terribly. We didn't have parachutes, but I thought it would be better to just land a little bit safely than us exploding from the impact.

I am you.

I tried to focus on the flying teachings I've been taught… from 'A Flying Jatt' movie. "What the hell are you doing?" She was laughing mid-air and not even *trying* so she'd know how hard it was.

We were about to approach the town and I still didn't have any plan on how I should take my entry; that wasn't the case with Kritika though, she curled into a ball and the very next second she unfolded all her limbs… two **giant** golden wings emerged from her back, shining like gold and looked like blessings of Goddess Durga… she was a literal Phoenix at that time.

It drastically reduced her velocity while I was still planning what to do… until I had a brilliant idea.

I extended my arm out, giving me full Young Thor chills. I reached the altitude of the highest building in the town; in precisely four seconds my face will be in the road. I heard a soothing whine, constantly increasing and right before the one second mark to reaching the ground, my sword was in my hands. I could feel its weight- real, powerful, buzzing with energy. Just like Mjolnir.

Kartikeya Sharma.

"Ha! I knew it! This is **SO** Goddamn awesome!" My sword was pulling me through the city roads *just* like Thor and *just* like I've liked it. I've used Mjolnir many times in dreams, but this was **just INCREDIBLE!**

I looked behind and she was catching up to me, we both were like Thor and Falcon, or in this case Phoenix… her wings were looking absolutely beautiful, big and glowing in the night sky. I was cutting through the thin air and the city atmosphere; I held onto the leather strap for a better grip, and I think after that my speed just increased even more.

With this speed I was about to reach the end of the town.

"Shall we land?" I asked her,

"Why? It's so fun!" she was tripping, I just slowed down and landed my feet on the ground, she looked very confused and upon the next thing, I laugh till this day, she crashed into a building.

She was partly embedded in it, and I was laughing like a mad man in the middle of the town. I looked around and

I am you.

the town was no different than mine, but I noticed many familiar faces except they were of opposite genders.

She walked beside me after a while, "Told ya to land" I teased her to which she didn't reply.

We both started walking across the town, she was looking around for known people and after moving by the next building two girls approached Kritika and started asking where she was… they were suspiciously familiar.

I glanced at Kritika, "Don't be surprised, they are Aadvi and Neha… **our** friends" My jaw dropped looking at them, both were girls but exactly the same body and facial features, talking style, humor and even the fact that Aadvi and Kritika roast up Neha like me and Aditya.

"This is absolutely crazy" although they were *actually* parts of her dream; her unconscious mind, it was so eerie and unbelievable.

I looked around and slowly but surely, I was able to recognize many people… Hitanshi, Suman, Aviral, Pranav, Shaurya, Yash and many more. All were perfectly recognizable even in opposite genders. Kritika slowly stepped besides me, *"This,* is my world" I looked around in awe, the people were known but weren't at the same time.

"Oh, look!" she pointed her figure to a person, I looked at him carefully and it was none other than Nandini of this world. "What's his name?" I asked while studying him.

"Nirbhay… Nirbhay Rathore"

"I am going to talk to him, it's a dream, they are like NPCs… let's see how he's like a boy" she hesitated as if trying to stop me but deeper inside she wanted me to talk to her, I knew it. I was the same gender as him, so I hope I'll have an easy time talking to him.

"Namaste my friend" I have no idea why I used this greeting when I could've used anything else, I guess I *am* very cultural. "Uh Namaste, how can I help you?" he asked in a very normal and casual tone, just like Nandini would say it.

"So, I am a friend of Kritika's, my name is Krishay, and I'd like to tell you that she'd *really* want to

I am you.

go out with you" I kept it like we've been friends forever.

He was *really* surprised to listen to this news. I had two reasons why I said this… first I wanted to see if the dream Nirbhay was like the real-life Nirbhay and would actually respond like it and not like some programmed goon. Second, if it *is* like real life and if he *actually* like Kritika… that'd mean that Nandini like me too… **in real life!**

Before he could say, I pointed towards her across the street, "There she is, just nervous to say this on her own, don't take it seriously though alright? Many people are"

He was looking really confused… he looked at her then me like three to four times. His friends, whom I suppose I of which was Vaishnavi were giggling. They made me confused as well.

"What do you mean go out with you? She's, my **girlfriend!**" My jaw dropped… I looked at her and she was asking what was happening, in sign language. I replied back… in sign language as the traffic made it impossible to communicate through words.

"He says you are his girlfriend, what is this about?" I learned sign language for a talent show in fifth grade, I thought I'd use it nowhere at that time. I was completely wrong. I never thought in 2019 that I'd use this skill to talk to myself apparently and in this amazing and crazy dream world.

She froze in place… unable to process what I just said, so she wanted me to repeat what I just tried to say,

"He says *you* are *his* girlfriend! You two… are *together*… understand me?"

She tripped on her own feet, and I rushed towards her to support her. I grabbed her from behind, Nirbhay was running to help her as well. She asked me to make him stop. I left her, stood in front of him and stretched my hand, the sword came in my empty palm, and I extended it towards him.

The people were taking photos of us like it was a movie shooting in the middle of the road. I was in my

I am you.

jacket and jeans, holding an energy-radiating blue-silver sword towards a simple, although a bit handsome guy in sweatpants and a T-Shirt. I could see the intense fear on his face, as if he'd pee his pants.

"Oh my God! Not like *that* Krish! Leave that right now!" Her voice came from behind, I could hear her standing on the ground again. I slowly lowered the sword and honestly if I used this majestic weapon for the Scorpion gang, they wouldn't stand more than five seconds on their best defense.

Now the funniest thing I experienced in that dream was that when I put down my sword, he just forgot what just happened.

"Kritika, are you alright, what happened? What did Krishay say to you in those symbols that made you fall on the ground?"

It was the *most* unconcerned voice I've ever heard. Like he didn't even care about her, just asking for formality. In my first thought I became extremely excited that Nandini would also have the same feelings for me… but after *this*? It's better if I just let Rupali kiss me, at least she's concerned about me unlike her.

"Yea I am okay leave that, did you just say we both are in relationship?" she was going crazy about it, but I didn't need to worry… if I thought that he was a bit out of line then she'd know this as well.

"I mean yes… we went out, we know each other's feelings and now we meet every day." This dream has its own fricking story line.

"Why do you sound so uninterested then?" Aha! There she is… I was enjoying the show, resting against a light pole.

"If you think I am *uninterested…* I shouldn't be wasting my time here worrying about you."

"Just go before I burn you alive" she walked away before he could say anything. I gave Nirbhay my signature two finger salute of goodbye.

"I can't believe he'd be in a relationship just for the sake of being in one. I put so many efforts just to get his attention and I know this is a dream but even in real life it's like he just ignores me, just wants someone to cut his time with be it anyone… like you understand what I am saying right?"

I am you.

I gave her the most sarcastic nod ever. "Oh, yea I sometimes forget I don't need to tell you anything about my life." While completing the sentence she was already clinging to my arm. We both looked into each other's eyes, once again.

"So where to now?"

"We have the whole town to roam around, or we could just..." she paused, "Just what?"

"Oh, come on you know what I am thinking!" she was on point. We said it together,

A road trip in an RV!

We both jogged our way to an empty parking lot, we spawned a big RV. It was not those old American ones... it was a Coachmen RV Pursuit 27XPS... one of the best in the world. We entered inside, and our eyes fell in our hands.

There was a kitchen, a couch, a bathroom and even a *bed!* I hopped onto the driver's cabin, and she just jumped on the bed.

Kartikeya Sharma.

"Ready?" I asked with a small horn.

"Let's take this house on wheels for a tour."

"Let's go!" I said shifting the gear.

I am you.

Chapter 11

-Our world. Our wish

I slowly pulled out of the parking lot and drove through the roads of the town. The main difference I saw between mine and her town was that mine had less lights and was like a town made in Minecraft. Hers was more like a city with lights and cars… like the times square. I wonder why my town is different than hers.

I mean I have to complain, mine's just simple and quiet and… simple. Although it's not like mine, it is so backward we don't even have fresh water, I mean I hope so. This town looked so busy like there were lights, decorations and everything. Although there weren't any advertisements because there wasn't anything like profit, loss, businesses, taxes, commissions or anything else.

My town people look like they live in a peaceful city and her town people live in a noisy city but still peacefully. That is till we arrived here as upon entering we made an impression on a building and a person peed his pants. We soon reached the edge of the town, and we were again roaming in this endless terrain.

As soon as I drove about fifty to hundred meters from the town, all the noise and chatters just blended in the background. It was me, her, this big machine and the cosmos above us. There was no road, no destination, just a large ground to drive on.

The RV had a nice scent of fresh leather and aroma of wood. The seat was really comfortable, my own personal big seat and no traffic in front of me.

"It's good that our knowledge to vehicles doesn't limit to just sports cars otherwise I hadn't seen any mobile phones here, we wouldn't be able to search up this beauty anywhere."

"You're *so* right, this sofa is so good."

"You do realize this thing has a queen size bed in the back, right?"

"**Oh, right** I *totally* forgot!" I heard her getting up from the sofa and jumping on the bed. "This is *so* soft and big! I could literally stay in this vehicle forever. No need for an expensive house."

"You do know vehicles lose value and houses usually gain it?"

"Yes, I know it but come one if you can move your house anywhere and don't have to pay any mortgage and the taxes will be extremely low compared to a full house."

"Yea I guess you are right" I was starting to consider her idea, maybe after college I'll just live in a RV, pay off the loan and live peacefully.

"Hey, turn up some music, it's getting a bit boring now" she was right. It can be boring when we just drive in a seemingly endless land with some highlands and that's all. "You're right let's have some fun."

I turned on cruise control at 80 kmph and went near the sofa. I turned on the TV and searched for some songs. I searched for the party songs which I listen to some nights when in a happy mood. All in Hindi and all placed in the top of my list. I started vibing and moving my legs around in the starting music of the song. She got up from the bed and started vibing as well.

"This song is one of my favorites" she held my shoulders, and I held her waist really firmly, "I know… it's my favorite too."

My voice went in a soft whisper as our faces leaned in. Her breath was warm against my skin, we were moving in a slow dance. We were half a finger away from each other and our eyes began to close. In a swift moment we jumped back, leaned in again with wide open eyes… singing the lyrics of the chorus of song out loud. We were dancing like we did at our uncle's wedding seven years ago. I am very shy when it comes to dancing, and I never dance in front of people, but this was like dancing in front of a mirror… which I usually do when I am alone in the house. We were singing the lyrics, dancing just like the lead dancer of the music video did, holding hands, looking into each other's eyes while singing it.

The RV ran over a little obstacle, and it resulted in a big jerk, apparently the suspension of this vehicle is the one thing which it is not praised for. I tried to make

I am you.

myself stable by holding the edge of the sofa, but she fell right on top of me.

We both were on the floor of an unsupervised moving vehicle which if flipped over would be a nightmare for us.

"Uh, so when exactly are you planning to stand up?" I asked with a raised eyebrow. She was zoned out the whole time *while* she was looking at me.
"Oh, uh right I should- get up, look at the road" She immediately went to the driver's seat and started redirecting the RV about 10 o'clock from our directing since apparently, we were driving in an abandoned farmland.

"I am locking the speed at 60 and it should be just fine" she stood up from the seat and we started dancing again. Sometimes we were doing the roleplays like we were *in* song and sometimes we just vibed on the parts of music where it's not as energetic.

After a while we both sat on the dinette from exhaustion. I looked behind and we were nearing a small town.

Kartikeya Sharma.

"I guess we have to stop and see what this town contains." I stood up and hopped into the driver's seat. I slowly stopped near a small house at the start of the town.

"Let's go see who lives in this small place." When we got out, we found out it was a lot smaller than we thought. It just had some small houses and a big garage in the middle.

"I don't get it who lives here, there are less than twenty houses here with no supply for food or anything" she had a valid point, the houses were fully furnished. We walked through the houses and by the time we were reaching the garage, we were starting to think it was another abandoned town.

"There's nothing here, shall we go?"

"Yea I guess, I am tired so I may use the bed" I smirked at her.

"You do realize we only have one bed, right?"

"Yup, one *double* bed…" we both stopped and looked into each other's eyes.

The last one to reach the RV sleeps on the couch!

I am you.

We both rushed to the RV when a deep masculine voice emerges behind us, "Stop… *right* now!"

We both came to a full stop and turned back in confusion. The garage door opened. There were not one, not two, not ten, not twenty but about *fifty* big, muscular people with skin filled with tattoos more than flesh.

They all wore ripped off t shirts and jackets and blue jeans… except one of them was just in his underpants.

We slowly stepped closer to them because for the time being we didn't have any fear for them.

"Can we help you guys?" she asked as if this was our home, and they were the intruders.

"Can you help… **us**?" one of them said this and I *totally* agree with him. "You two, are not going out of here without being cut into a million pieces which even the Vultures will refuse to feed on."

He said it in the deepest and cough filled voice we have ever heard out of a man… or any person actually and all I could ask think of to say to him was, "There are vultures here?"

Kartikeya Sharma.

Kritika giggled a bit but apparently those guys didn't like it. They all started gathering all kinds of melee weapons.

Brass knuckles, batons, machetes, clubs, cleavers, crowbars and these were only picked by the weak and small ones. The big dudes took big axes, mallets and sledges. The most dangerous was the leader, he took a *huge* Lumber axe which I could see was made of obsidian. They were all slowly walking towards us.

"Oh boy this is going to be fun" I replaced my jacket with a sleek but powerful armor, it had glowing blue lines everywhere, it was radiating with energy. My shoes turned into boots extending to my shins and just so they don't behead me, my collar was high till the back of my neck.

"I just hope this isn't the bullshit where we actually die if we die here" she also changed her clothes into a suit with different pieces of fabric on them… radiating blue just like mine and she tied her hair in a ponytail.

My mind started to go back to a really specific point where I saw her this way,

I am you.

My sketch.

I first imagined her in this armor… this *exact* armor. My thoughts were making no sense, I didn't even know her at that point.

They were approaching us, preparing to tear every flesh off our skeleton, I was a bit scared… it had more weight than a horror movie. We both extended our arms towards our back and after a few moments my sword came with a loud whine right into my hands, radiating with the same blue energy as my suit.

A while later her axe came as well, with the same bustling energy as my sword. We were both ready to take the fight which we didn't expect we'd get. Although after what we *have* experienced here, this shouldn't be a surprise to us.

Before charging we cried out an unplanned yet perfect battle cry.

It's our world and it's our wish here!

Chapter 12

-Fight for fun

They all charged at us in one motion. They all were shouting loudly, and the thudding of steps made the stuff inside the houses shake.

They were all furious, as if a bee entered their garage and never left, or they hit their small toe finger on a table or they pulled a *very* long hang nail. I did it back in third grade, my skin just peeled like a sticker till my knuckle.

That was painful…

I shouted like a dead duck in my class and honestly my teacher was relieved that I didn't turn into a warewolf in the open day.

"Stop right now!" she shouted as hard as she could to stop them for a thing we always wished to do before a big fight or in an intense moment. It was cool, but hey, let's be honest, I've got a deeper voice.

I am you.

They were almost about to reach us. "Do something!"

"Alright!" I took two small steps.

Stop... RIGHT now!

My voice did it. They all stopped like a K9 getting orders from his commander. As soon as they stopped, Kritika spawned a boom box like it was in her back pocket this whole time.

She put it down and I pulled out a cassette tape... out of air and put it in the boom box. A boom box because we don't have a mobile phone to connect it to a Bluetooth speaker.

We don't even know if the phone will work because I see no network towers... although we did turn on the TV but who cares, we are in front of giant people with no guns thankfully. The guys were looking at us with frustrated looks. The music started slowly... it had a long duration of very light music but as soon as the lyrics started, we both started vibing.

Kartikeya Sharma.

"Ma-I-A Hi" I made an exaggerated expression while saying this. She repeated after me, "Ma-I-A Hu." The guys were getting really pissed we were vibing on 'Dragostea din tei' a song released more than a decade ago. After the beat drop, we were just dancing at that point.

"Ma-I-A Hi… Ma-I-A Hu… Ma-I-A Ho… Ma-I-A Ha-Ha…"

And with that they charged at us with, now even more furious than before… I guess we made a mistake but nothing and I mean *nothing* can convince us to do a job without having fun.

Seriously, one of them screamed so loud, I think a bird fell out of the sky somewhere.

They all charged again, fists up, eyes burning like they just saw someone scratch their new car, or truck or whatever they drive.

I spun my sword in the air, re-gripped it tightly and started walking towards them. Kritika dragged her axe through her chest making a scratch on it. Not sure why, but it looked cool.

I am you.

"Let's gooo!" I shouted and ran straight into the middle guy. He was *so* huge; he looked like he ate children. I ducked under his punch and slapped his back so hard I think he got confused and said "Huh?" out loud.

Kritika jumped up, wrapped her legs around some other guy's neck like it was a wrestling match, and twisted. He spun, she spun, both spun and they both fell — but she landed like a cat, and he landed like a potato sack.

Another guy ran towards me with a crowbar. Although it would be pretty dangerous, it wasn't a competition for what rested in my hands… I spun my sword with the handle and with a spin shot his crowbar was in two pieces now. Till he realized what happened I gave a light thrust with one hand his Jello like stomach had a huge hole.

Someone tried to grab Kritika from behind, but she stepped aside, jumped and delivered a slash with her axe right to his chest… as he was too tall for her to behead him.

Kartikeya Sharma.

My sword kept releasing energy with every hit, I walked into the group and just kept slashing around, I was surrounded by them. "Ouu… someone finally managed to stab a fire axe right below my shoulder. I turned around and with the momentum slashed that guy into two pieces.

"Wait… why is there *barely* any blood? It's not like it's a little scratch I am causing them" it made no sense but since they were not walking up, I was sure they were dead.

She was doing all sorts of aerial attacks… spins, jumping, climbing on them, thrusting a person by jumping from another person's body. In summary she was moving with the wind, or maybe it's the complete opposite.

"Shall we do something cool? I mean it's not like we will lose but let's have fun of this dream. Even though these dudes don't deserve them" she said while blocking a sledgehammer attack from a dude.

We both backed up a bit, the leader looking at us from the back of the group. I stuck my sword in the

I am you.

ground, held her legs and started spinning her as fast as I could. She was holding the axe in her hands.

One of the guys jumped high to attack us from the top.

Kritika let go of the axe, I let go of her and raised my sword in the sky, and as expected, he fell right onto the blade.

"Ugh, not doing that again, gross" I let go of my hand, he was *so* heavy my arm would've been turned to literal bone meal.

I looked in front and the axe was spinning with more momentum than I gave it, piercing and slashing everything and everyone which came in its way. Kritika just crashed into a house and was recovering herself.

I laughed at her, "You alright peanut?" She was still tumbling, which to be honest I was too. The axe went right by the head of the leader…

"Oh… just missed it" I said in regret.

"Not anymore" she said while extending her arm, the axe traced its path back to Kritika, but the leader held onto it and just broke it with his Lumber axe.

Kartikeya Sharma.

"Get aside!" he shouted to all the dudes who were left as if it was our doom already, He ran towards her, and she had no weapon on her… nor the time to think and create a new weapon. He ran and leaped like the Hulk; his Lumber axe was high, ready to cut her in half.

She crouched down, screaming for her life. I rushed in front of her just in time, raising my sword to block his axe. He wasn't just some random thug, had a thick beard, short hair, and his breath reeked of alcohol. I rested my knee on the ground, but it was no help, he pushed with both hands, I could see small cracks forming on the blade of my sword.

I wasn't able to say a single word, my face was red, even a tiny breathe in could've ended me… or this dream I suppose but it wasn't sure. I dropped the sword and jumped back, he slashed, and my stomach was badly injured, he sliced through my armor like a piece of cake and made a huge cut below my last rib.

Heal

I am you.

Heal

Heal!

"Why does it take *this* long to heal, I'd die till the time my body decided to help me" I wasn't some X-man… I had no idea how my arm healed before.

I was trying to get away from him but then I heard a loud battle cry… Kritika extended her hand, my sword went to her, and she began a 1v1 with him. He was receiving no damage, no injury whatsoever as if she was fighting with an obsidian rock itself.

Every one of her attacks was easily blocked by his axe.

He made a huge strike, and my sword was broken as well… she flied back a bit from the energy which released.

"First you, and then this dude…" he slowly walked towards her… I was looking at the scene although my vision was too blurry.

"He, is me… you injured him, means you injured **me**" I've never even seen myself as furious as I saw her at that moment. Her hair started to flow, defying gravity… or any other rule which exists here.

She started floating above the ground. The guy got scared for the first time as he stepped back… Golden light rays were gleaming from her body. Her armor got fixed and her broken axe went back to her and piece by piece it became a one piece and then transformed into a huge… golden… Trishul.

Her phoenix wings came back, and I could see the very Goddess in her… which I was not surprised that she was her devotee. I looked at her in awe, many a times I've encountered some Gods in my dreams, but this was just breath taking…

Fabulous!

He started to retreat; the other guys were already gone till the time he moved like a block ahead. He turned back and grinned… in a sudden moment he turned back and threw his Axe towards her.

I am you.

As soon as it reached her, she grabbed it, spun and threw it right back at back at him. He barely dodged it.

I was starting to heal, and I think at the same time… her powers were going, she was beginning to lose balance midair, and the glow was slowly decreasing.

He saw the scene and ordered everyone to go and kill me. "Kritika!" I shouted after getting on my feet. I raised my hand, and she dropped the Trishul in my hand and within moments, without taking any aim I threw it past the crowd and the prongs pierced through his neck… knocking him down for good.

It flew back to me and with the spear head on its other side I thrusted it into the earth and rested my leg on one of its rings towards the bottom.
Not bragging but I am quite intimidating myself… if I have this powerful weapon anyone will fear for its life. I didn't get any wings or glows though… "I wanted to fly like Kritika."

On this thought I realized and looked up just in time for her wings to disappear completely. I rushed towards her and caught her in my arms. She was looking at me, I was looking at her…

She held my face and looked through it, "Are you alright?" I asked her. She immediately clung to me like a teddy bear and began crying…

"I thought I'd lose you" her words were unclear due to the sniffing in between; her tears were flowing down my armor…

Right next to our RV I moved my hands, the materials and stuff from the houses of town began flying like toy pieces and it made a big enough cabin. I walked inside it and gently put her on the bed.

She was groaning with pain like me, I somehow removed her armor and despawned mine. We both lay flat on the bed, breathing heavily. "This… was not easy."

She wept her tears and agreed with me. We were dirty, sweaty and even bloody in some places.

"So, you just want to come out clean or take a bath?" I asked her.

I am you.

"You already know the answer Sharma" I indeed did.

"Who will go in the shower first?" she asked after a while. "Both of us can go at the same time" her head immediately turned towards me. Her face was a mixture of confusion and a slight smile.

"Oh, hey don't get all excited, this cabin has two bathrooms" she took a breath of relief in an attempt to show she wasn't happy with what I just said before this.

We both were flat on our backs on the bed for a while… All I could think of was, "Who is she really?" After seeing her form when I was injured, I seriously considered thinking this. Although asking it didn't seem right, I don't know why.

Chapter 13

-Me, you and the world

"Ok… I am going now, will rest after getting a hot shower." She groggily stood up and went inside the first door and locked it. I woke up, tried to wash away my thoughts and went to the second bathroom. It was big enough with a large bathtub, cupboard sink and toilet. There was still plenty of space to walk around and even dance, which I sometimes do in my house.

I took off *all* my clothes, closed the drain and turned on hot water. Till the time it was filling up I started to move my legs around in the bathroom. I heard a knock on the wall, I went near it to see what was up.

"You are dancing as well huh?" she asked from the other bathroom.

"Yea what is it to you? I bet you're dancing as well" I know she can't see me but whenever someone disturbs me in the bathroom it makes me feel uncomfortable.

I am you.

"Yes, I was, just wanted to check in how you are doing" this made no sense... like who actually asks question like these?

Ok to be fair I sometimes ask my brother so I guess I shouldn't be surprised if she does it.

"Just go already why tub is almost full."

"Mine too... catch you later." She left after that. "Finally, some peace and quietness. I slowly lowered my feet in the tub, the water was perfectly warm. I slowly sat in and rested my head against one end of it.

"Oh, my I've not been in a tub since like fifteen months now." It was weird that I was bathing inside a dream, and it was actually feeling so relaxed. I won't even *try* to pee in the toilet because everyone knows what happens after that. It has happened to me quite a lot of times now and I won't fall for it again, not in *this* dream.

I was wondering about the fast how long this dream is compared to any of my other dreams. I turned on the shower on the ceiling above my head. It was as if I am sitting in a warm lake under a waterfall. All my fatigue and pain just vanished.

Well, it was already gone after we hopped on the bed, but this was just giving me happiness and relaxation. I took the soap and washed my body. The water was now dirty, so I drained it and washed my body with the shower.

After washing everything I got out of the tub and somehow spawned everything I wanted.

I got out of the bathroom; she was still inside… "Drying her hair for sure." I sat on the bed, thinking about my feelings for her. I've never found anyone like her, not Nandini, not Rupali, not *anyone*. I remembered the little moment we had in the mall… for the first time I thought I was actually close to someone.

She listens to me, well only sometimes since she knows everything about me, obviously… she is beautiful yet daring, like me, she's funny and good in studies, her humor is just like me… of course all of it was true, she *is* me.

I couldn't find anyone who would be a better partner for me than her. We sync up so well, *literally*. We are so unpredictable for others but know exactly what the other will say or do.

I am you.

She knows everything I know, sketching, sign language, parkour and even has the same music taste as me. She is *just* perfect.

I stood up and looked through the window. Towards my right in the sky, the Event Horizon, it had changed its position again. I got concerned about how much time we really have with each other. Suddenly the door creaked open, and she came out in a light T-shirt and jeans.

"Ready? Let's go" she was confused, "Where are we going?" she asked reluctantly.

"Somewhere special" I said while changing my clothes to a hoodie and a track pants. She jumped on the bed, "I want to relax a bit." She said this in the cutest voice possible, but I knew it was a honey trap… I picked her up from the bed. Her cheeks turned red, and she exclaimed like she didn't know I was going to do this.

Outside ground was full of bodies and our broken boombox. There was barely any blood though.

Kartikeya Sharma.

The Trishule was still there, stuck in the ground in an upright position.

I opened the door and took her to the RV. I gently placed her on the bed, locked the door, started the vehicle and drove it towards the direction we came from. She was sleeping on the bed, I didn't know you could do that in a dream… what if she had a dream inside of the dream? Can you even do that?

I had a lot of questions, but I just kept driving. Not even five minutes in and she wakes up saying now she feels extremely energetic and active.

"This dream logic is out of my bounds… it's too much to understand here."

She just sat on the sofa and looked outside, just lost in thought, as if trying to make sense of this thing.

"Everything okay? You seem lost." I asked while looking at her in the rearview mirror. She smiled but didn't look at me, her eyes were fixed outside.

"I never thought I'd find someone like you, especially in this crazy dream. After going out with

I am you.

Nirbhay I started to doubt my choice but ever since I found out you are just me from another world, I never thought of him even once. The crazy thing is I have no idea how long this will continue or if this is even real or not."

She put me in a deep thought. Every one of her words drilled a deep hole in my mind.

She was right.

I want her more than anything, but it was not possible and the change in the position of the two worlds in the sky is probably our time limit in this place. I looked in front of me, suddenly slammed the brakes and slowly pulled over.

"We have come to our destination Mrs. Sharma" I said while getting off the seat. I drive us to the seacoast, where we first realized we were something more than just entities in each other's dreams.

"It's beautiful." I said, "Never got a chance to properly see it when we first arrived here."

Kartikeya Sharma.

It was truly beautiful, the crystal-clear water, the cosmos and the horizon itself. We both went near the water and just stood there for a while. She spawned a large mattress… a *really* large one. We took our shoes off and sat on the thin mattress.

There was no sun, no moon, no dawn, no dusk. Just us two in front of this endless ocean. We both looked at each other, her cascade was covering her face due to the wind. They were not too long and not too short, just perfect wavy hair till the shoulders.

I am supposing she is thinking about my looks as well.

"You know, I suppose I won't be needing Nandini or anyone now that I know you exist somewhere in the world."

I said in a very low voice; it was starting to make me blush.

"Wait so what about the marriage? If you say you are married to yourself, they'll probably just bring a random girl and make you marry her… you know we *hate* these kinds of marriages."

I am you.

"I mean yea but let's just forget the things coming up, what I see coming up is that we'll wake up in our own worlds and we'd never be able to see each other again."

"The worst thing you've done today is make me fall for you, now I don't even know till when I'll keep remembering you." Her eyes started to tear a bit but she somehow managed to not let a single drop spill.

She laughs, she knows I saw her hide her pain, "Don't worry, sometimes we just forget what we saw in dreams or if we even saw one." I just said this to cheer her up, I am not sure if I am right or not.

She gives a *very* obvious look, "You do know none of your bluffing will work on me, right?"

I looked back at the coast with a smile on my face, "I know."

We had an awkward silence in the middle, both were looking at the crystal-like shining water.

I tried to keep the conversation going, "What's your plan? What will you do after we wake up?"

Kartikeya Sharma.

She gave it a long thought and slightly pouted her lips in a kiss shape. "I have a blank mind on me. I think after waking up I'll be just, sitting… staring at something trying to remember if all this place any sense."

I added to her answer, "And since we slept on a rainy night, maybe go out for a walk to clear our mind."

"Yea a walk sounds nice. Seriously though last night was just *crazy* good." I looked at the sea again, "No doubt."

We sat in silence for some time again before she asked me a questing, "What will you do about this Nandini situation?" she had a valid question. I have **totally** fallen for Kritika right now.

She's cute, strong, badass, her thinking and pretty much everything is the same as mine, her looks are what attract me the most to girls. Her hair are perfect like I've noticed many times now, her black wavy hair ending right above the shoulders.

She's absolutely gorgeous, like I could see her whole day and would not get bored of it.

"So do you also like me, my looks specifically?" she asked me as I was thinking the same thing.

I am you.

"Of course I do, I am obsessed with my own looks, why wouldn't I be with yours?" she gave a shy smile, and it *melted* my heart! Seriously I can pull her into a hug *right* now.

"I think you are cute as well… or handsome maybe I don't know, I've never complimented a boy before, so I have absolutely no idea how to make it feel less weird or cheesy."

I chuckled, "You know I've never received such compliments in a meaningful way, specially from a girl. It's not like I am a dumb or ignored guy in school, just that I haven't interacted with girls as much as I have with boys…

And they are not the ones to give compliments, especially on looks."

She nodded her head in agreement, giving a low hum. She looked at me, I looked at her… our eyes fixed on ourselves technically like they always are when we look in a mirror.

Kartikeya Sharma.

"So shall we, do it?" her voice was trembled a little, "I was waiting for you to say it, let's go"

We stood up on the mattress and looked at each other. We were waiting for the moment to kick in, we had no rush right now, we wanted to enjoy it to the fullest.

We spread our arms.

Walked closer.

We moved our hands forward, instinctively wrapping them around each other. My left arm slid over her shoulder, gently cradling the back of her neck, while my right arm found its way beneath her left arm, pulling her body tightly against mine.

For some unknown reason my fists were closed.

She wrapped both of her hands around my neck unlike me and it gave me chills which spread across my body.

I felt a deep sense of comfort, warmth and unusual attraction towards her. I refused to let her go

I am you.

and she refused to let me go as well, I could feel her grip tightening.

"This feels so good and comforting." She said in a soft and sweet whisper. "Yea I'd do this anytime with you, hold you closer to me. It's like hugging myself because no one else is so close enough I can actually hug like this."

She agreed strongly, her arms shifting but not losing their grip.

I buried my face in her shoulder and closed my eyes completely, letting the feeling spread across my body, her scent was like honey to my nose.

After what felt like forever… we finally let go of each other, we wanted to hold each other again and I knew it. We sat on the mattress again and this time we completely lied down on our back, looking at the beautiful and absolutely marvelous sky, filled with constellations, galaxies, planets and most concerning… our two big universes which again had a different position and placement as last time.

Kartikeya Sharma.

I preferred not to say it… because the truth might break whatever spell was keeping us together, she might have already known it… trying not to say it to me. We just wanted to experience each other's presence with no worries about what to do next.

I glanced at her.

Glanced at her with a hidden eye so she doesn't suspect.

She was sitting in a chill, relaxed pose. One knee folded up and the other flat on the mattress. She was looking at the sea, probably thinking the same thing which I am thinking.

Her face was partly covered with her hair strands and partly with the soft glow of blue light from the sea.

Now that I think of it, Nandini doesn't even come close to how lovely Kritika is. When I saw her for the first time, I saw myself in her… which I do when I look in mirror.

I never saw anything as such in Nandini or any other girls. I guess I was just trying to list all the good qualities of Nandini and exaggerate them just because I like her.

I am you.

She was constantly looking at me with her side eye like I was. We both knew we were having chances glancing at each other, so I just looked at her and didn't turn my head away.

The next time she tried to look at me, she just turned her head completely towards me after she saw me admiring her.

For the next four minutes we were just sitting and not saying anything. She was the one to break the silence, "How do you feel like loving yourself?"

I thought for a while before answering, "Well, it's nothing like constantly gazing yourself in mirror everyday… every hour actually. It's like I am meeting myself, which technically I am, but I can now see myself from my own perspective… it is nice and absolutely incredible."

By the last line my lips curved in a smile, and she gave a sheepish little chuckle. The comfort of the mattress was a nice touch at this moment where my stomach was filled with butterflies.

"Having a funny stomach?" I asked her and without even listening to the question, she replied, "So much I don't know what to do about it."

We slowly moved closer to each other, adjusting our sitting position a little. We held eye contact for a while, both of our eyes were studying each other's faces, as if searching for something in it.

"I never thought I'd look *this* handsome as a guy." She continued, "Like your hair, your face cut; I mean it's the same as mine to be honest… your beautiful eyes, smooth lips often tugged into a cocky grin just like mine."

I continued with her lines, "your thick eyebrows, flushing cheeks which always get red in front of me…"

She had a little grin at that line but just as I expected, they were red as a rose once again.

"Honestly I never thought I'd be this beautiful as a woman myself." I cupped her cheek with my right hand. She started to well up a little, looking at me in great awe, her head tilted a little to the left.

I am you.

She slowly moved closer to me, her eyes lowed and tears ran down her cheek. My hands instinctively lowered as she came closer. In a moment our lips meet, my eyes closed on their own, this feeling was different, a little weird, it was something different… but it was nice, something neither of us has experienced.

For a while we just stood there, our hands lowered and our lips touching. Just about three seconds after she pulled back slightly, her head was down and then up, looking into my eyes.

My eyes started to tear up as well, I wiped them away and smiled at her.

Thank you.

She said in a really low whisper, "You've completely changed me, thank you for that."

I smiled at her and then leaned again. This time we both smiled and with a little unfinished giggle, our lips met again.

It was just us, one soul in two bodies, joined by a little dream.

157

Chapter 14

-Despertar Sin Ti

We both pulled away and this time our lips curved in a little smile; we were happy to have each other. For a while we just stood there, "So what to do now?" she asked.

I was clueless, standing there just like that. I started to notice her height was a little weird for me. I am taller than most of the girls in my class, and Nandini is a whole head shorter than me.

She was *exactly* my height, no looking down anymore… It was a little weird, it's hard to find a 5 foot 9 inches tall girl in my school or my locality. It was a nice change in the usual habit. I wonder if she's a tall girl in her world, probably yes.

I looked around the world and saw something unusual across the sea. The horizon, it was being eaten it… by the world itself. A black shadow covered and

I am you.

engulfed anything which came in its way. We both were tense and together we looked up at the universe, it was not beautiful anymore, they were absolutely out of line, nothing parallel about them anymore.

We both looked at each other, "Our time has come." We both said together. We looked towards the sea again, it was coming fast, we had little to no time left. "We have to go now!" she exclaimed while holding my hand to run.

As soon as our feet touched the sand, our feet were covered by shoes, and we ran to a high land. We saw the shadow advancing with great pace. "It's our time, there's no denying in it now." I said it to her, my heart was aching, as if I myself was about to die right now.

We both looked at each other, her eyes were filled with tears, so were mine. She cupped my face with her right hand.

"I don't want to lose you." She said while crying. I couldn't stop my tears, but I can surely put a smile on.

"You won't, I am you… we'll always stay together, and no dream or universe can separate us from this truth."

She wiped her tears and so did I, we both leaned in and kissed on final time before we get separated, it was filled with a closure, acceptance and a deep emotional meaning.

We are **one** and no one can change that reality.

After what felt like the whole eternity, we pulled away, our foreheads were resting against each other. Our tear-filled eyes saw a blurry reflection of each other in front of us,

I love you.

She said in a poetic and soft voice, barely above a whisper… it was everything I could've lived with, it was enough.

"And I you."

"Krishay?" I answer with a soft hum, "If you find someone in your world who looks like me, talk to them, maybe it's me waiting for you."

Her words carried so much weight and desperation, at this point I didn't care if I had to live without her, this dream is enough to keep me awake and alive.

I am you.

The shadow reached the coast, engulfing our RV. We both held each other in our arms for the last time, our tears were soaking in each other's shoulders. Suddenly I felt a really hard and painful sensation.

I was losing her, for real this time.

My heart weighed heavy with this single thought, I couldn't let go of the only person I don't want to live without. I had no other choice than this, this is our fate, nothing can change it now.

The shadow began climbing the highland, we both pulled away, our eyes filled with tears, but our lips curved in a bittersweet smile.

Suddenly the ground had no contact with our feet, our bodies started to feel lighter and lighter. Soon we were floating in the air, completely out of our control, none of our powers were working.

The darkness slowly spread in front of our eyes, and we began to slowly fade away. In unison, we both did our two-finger farewell salute as she vanished from my sight. I closed my eyes and let the world take me wherever it's taking me.

Kartikeya Sharma.

I opened my eyes after a while, I was floating in the cosmos itself, in the middle of all the space we saw from the ground below.

This is beautiful…

I looked around and there was no one. I tried to find Kritika, but I had no clue about her. I saw a little light source, like a very tiny star. I floated towards the light and as I went closer to it the white light covered my sight. I extended my hand.

With a bright flash, and a sudden jerk, I was up in my bed, my own bed in my own bedroom. I looked around to examine the place like it was my first time here. I was covered in a blanket, a thick mattress behind my head and my pillow to my side.

"It's over after all" I whispered.

The though lingered in my mind for quite a while, I just sat there like a statue, trying to remember when I slept or what all happened during the dream.

I could barely remember anything…

The memories of that dream, that experience, those sights… everything was slowly vanishing. "I can only

I am you.

remember one person, a girl I suppose but… I cannot remember her face. What was her name, her name… I am pretty sure I spent my entire night with her in some place with her."

It was getting really frustrating… I slammed my nightstand, Come on, Krish! You've got to remember her… that place, those moments."

It was no use… I couldn't remember a single thing.

"I promised myself to never forget her." I looked down beside my lap, there was the sketch I was making last night. I hesitated to pick it up, but I did it anyway.

Kritika.

I saw the sketch, a beautiful woman who was strikingly similar to whom I met in the dream, but I still couldn't remember what she exactly looked like, what all things we did or even if we did it or not. "This cannot be a simple ordinary dream, I know something's behind it."

I tried really hard to remember, Nothing. Empty. My mind was completely blank. "I swear she was someone more than a person in my dream." Tears started to fall from my cheeks.

"Why am I crying over this?" nothing was making sense at that time, I decided to let it go for now and stood up from my bed, my feet were heavy, and my mind was racing. I checked the time and to my surprise, it was only 8:07 a.m. "I woke up *this* early. The night felt like I have been sleeping for months."

Suddenly the cold wind got hold of me, I started shivering in my pajamas. I went closer to the window and opened the curtains, there was no sign of the sun anywhere, dark clouds filled the sky, and it was still raining though not as much as last night.

"It is so beautiful." There was something about that day which felt unusually good… yesterday afternoon was literally burning and now it's as if the season changed in a single day. I stood there, watching the water droplets splash on the ground, the roadsides were filled with water streams and thin sheets of ice.

Frost covered the leaf ends of small plants and the edges of windshields of cars. The sky was clear white with clouds filling the gaps, it didn't feel like a normal 8

I am you.

a.m. morning. It had been a long time since I've seen this kind of morning.

I turned on the lights in my room and started making my bed. I picked up the sketch and admired it. A little smile appeared on my face, "Maybe it *was* a normal dream after all."

I closed the sketch book and put it on my table. This Sunday morning was about enjoying, not taking any kind of tension. I went down to see my parents on the couch enjoying the weather with chai and light romantic music playing from the speakers.

"Good morning mom and dad." I greeted them while walking past the hall to the bathroom. "Good morning Krish, did you look outside? You should go out for a walk."
"That's the plan dad." I went inside the bathroom and picked up my custom toothbrush, custom being I drew wolverine on its handle with markers.

I washed my face and looked in the mirror, I noticed something unusual, "I look… different. I am not sure what I am missing but it doesn't feel like me form

165

last night, something feels out of place, maybe my face is… whiter."

I left it as it was and started brushing. My mind was constantly flickering between last night and the previous day. The day was full of new things, hanging out with Nandini, change in the climate so abruptly, that relaxing and unusual night.

I somehow tried to get my mind off those things and by 8:39 a.m. I came out of the shower with a really cool body. I bathe with cold water in this cold climate, it was as if I was under a waterfall in the Himalayas.

"I won't use a hair dryer today, I'll let them air dry with time. Not feeling like properly styling up today."

I went to my room to wear a light hoodie and track pants. I just combed my hair without any oil and applied some light kajal as a Sunday special. I hurried down the stairs to see if there is something in breakfast, the table and kitchen seemed empty.

"Mom there's no breakfast today?" I asked from the dining room.

I am you.

"No son the power is out since last night, plus I thought you may go out to eat today."

An immediate smile radiated on my face, "Thank you *so much* ma." I went to the living room to hug her in between her newspaper reading session and rushed to my room.

"Okay so I need my earphones, money and my phone"

I quickly changed my clothes to a dark blue jean, a simple black US Polo T-Shirt and a black Shacket on top and before going out took a last glimpse of the sketch of Kritika on table.

I stood there for a while just in case I remembered something… nothing. I breezed past the door with earphones in my ears. The rain had stopped by that time.

"Oh Whoa!" I almost slipped while crossing the road. "That was a save; the roads are still slippery."

I went outside my locality and reached the town. I was walking past the cold breezes, vibing and hoping around on the beats of the song.

I was out on my own little adventure now…

Chapter 15

-First dawn with you

I was walking around without caring for anyone around me. I decided to go to 32 Apples again. I didn't take a short cut through an alley this time, I was planning to go all around the block.

The song ended and the next song which played made me remember some moments.

I got it!

It was the song I played somewhere, and I am pretty sure I danced on it, although I was having troubles where have I done it because I haven't danced in years now. The song played and I was constantly trying to remember what is going on.

Since this morning small flashbacks and unclear memories have been showing up, specially of that person, I know I had a dream, and it was… something.

I am you.

Slowly the song faded into background, and I was left in a deep thought, "Something isn't making sense, but I don't know what." I looked up in frustration, "I don't know how to find it out."

I almost reached the café, and I had no luck in trying to make out what happened last night.

"Ok Krishay… relax yourself, soon you'll forget what it was about. Let's just enjoy the sweet breakfast for now."

I was standing on the other side of the road where the café was situated. I removed my earphones and put them in my pocket. The place was being decorated for Christmas which wasn't a surprise… this store attracted the most customers during festive seasons.

"I am just waiting for the snow to come; it's almost December anyway and as per the last night's rain… I am pretty sure next precipitation will be in the form of snow."

The signal was red, and all the cars hauled to a stop. I, along with many people, started crossing the road. Upon reaching the store, the scent travelled right through my nose.

"Ah yes…" I took a long sniff. "I missed this scent." It was a mix of vanilla, chocolate and butter from pastries. I entered and the place was fairly empty, only a couple of people were sitting around.

"Hi Sharon! How's the work going?" I asked while approaching the counter. She turned back towards me, "Oh Hi Krishay!" she came out of the counter, "Enjoying the weather I see huh?" she hugged me which I didn't mind, she was a sweet lady, a year or two older than me at max.

"I'll have the chicken sandwich and a hot cocoa today along with the dark forest pastry." She started working on it instantly, "Coming right up."

I made my way to one of the seats beside the wall which had sofas instead of the usual chairs which were placed in the middle of the café. I sat down and checked my phone; I had a notification from Nandini.

Nandini: "Hi K! Yesterday we ate ice cream to get off the heat and today it's *this* cold… not lying I am sitting in bed all day, talking to Vaishnavi. What about you?"

I am you.

Replying back didn't seem like an option to me at the time for some reason, I just closed the phone and sat there waiting for my food.

I looked around, observed people, enjoyed the smell and most importantly tried *not* to think of these fading memories. I was thinking of what to do after getting home, or if I *am* going home. This weather will make it difficult for me to resist the outdoors.

"Just two more minutes Krishay!" Sharon told me from the counter, I nodded in compliance. I was thinking my own thoughts when suddenly in front of me I saw a girl.

She was sitting beside the other side of the café, reading a book. Something in me found a weird attraction towards her, an inner desire to approach her. She was wearing a parka with a fur hoodie and a muffler wrapped around the neck.

"She seems… similar… from somewhere." I examined her more, a light blue slim jeans and black boots. Her wavy cascade fell down to her shoulders and a big metal frame pair of glasses on her eyes.

Her sitting manner was elegant and comfortable, not giving any heed to the environment around her. Her eyes skimmed through the text, here light pink soft lips in a slight smile of happiness.

"I've seen her somewhere… she seems, too close to me, as if we have known each other for a long time."

Being the usual confident guy I am, I stood up and walked towards her. "What could possibly happen?"

I questioned myself, "Worst case she'll just say I am a creep or something." I kept walking towards her. My movement confident and my thoughts determined on finding out her identity.

I approached her table, "Excuse me miss." she looked at me. My eyes squinted a little and my mouth opened in utter shock. She had the *exact* same reaction. She put her book down and stood up from her chair. We were both in extreme disbelief and then it hit me.

"We both are of same height." I whispered.

I am you.

"We both have same hair type." She whispered as well.

"We both have the same face cut." I tilted my head.

"We both know exactly what the other is thinking right now." She tilted her head as well.

It was impossible, I was in front of a complete mirror of myself. My mind started racing and slowly, everything fell in place. The little flashbacks, the memories, the song, what all happened last night.

We kept standing there… my mind racing, heartbeat increased, legs shaking and all I could think I right now was, "How is this possible?"

We both took a step closer to each other, our faces inches apart from each other… those eyes, that was it, she was it, she *was* her.

We both said at the same time—

"Kritika?!"
"Krishay?!"

Author's Note.

The idea for this story originated from the anime "Your name". I heard of this anime in one of BeastBoyShub's videos. One night while listening to Die for You by STARSET, the whole story just started playing in my mind.

I am 16 years old as of now and I am really happy I am able to bring this whole story into existence. Writing was a lot of fun, specially the nights I had nothing to do but type this. This story is really close to me, and I had thought of this a year prior to when I started writing this.

It's not perfect and I am okay with it… it's filled with the emotions I carry. It's mine and it means the world to me.

If you've made it this far, thank you. Truly. You've given this story a voice by reading it, and that means everything.

-Kartikeya Sharma